William Fuller Bibliography
(1913–1982)

Novels
Brad Dolan series:
Back Country (Dell, 1954)
Goat Island (Dell, 1954)
The Girl in the Frame (Dell, 1957)
Brad Dolan's Blonde Cargo (Dell, 1957)
Brad Dolan's Miami Manhunt (Dell, 1958)
Tight Squeeze (Dell, 1959)

The Pace That Kills (Dell, 1956)

Stories
Bernie and Me (*Collier's*, Oct 25 1947)
Blind Man's Island (*Collier's*, May 17 1947)
Coondog's War (*Argosy*, July 1952)
Dog Man (*Adventure*, Feb 1949)
Early Rose and the High Sheriff (*Collier's*, Apr 1 1950)
Flight by Night (*Sky Aces*, Apr 1940)
The French Doll (*Collier's*, Dec 1 1951)
Full-Blooded Indian (*Collier's*, Mar 20 1948)
The Fun We Had (*McCall's*, Nov 1948)
The Good Land (*Collier's*, Jan 31 1953)
The Kidnapping (*Collier's*, Oct 11 1952)
A Lick for Brother Ed (*Collier's*, Mar 17 1951)
Life, Liberty and Orrin Dooley (*Collier's*, Dec 28 1946)
Mess with the Marshall! (*Collier's*, Jun 21 1952)
On the Linger (*Collier's*, Jan 6 1951)
Pillar of the Community (*Collier's*, Oct 6 1951)
Rabbity Boy (*Collier's*, May 10 1947)
Rattlesnake (*Adventure*, Oct 1948)
The Sheriff of Sunshine County (*Collier's*, May 10 1952)
Shoot Little Chicken (*Esquire*, Mar 1949)
Special Deputy (*Collier's*, Nov 8 1952)
Strangler Fig (*Collier's*, July 12 1947)
Tiger Swamp Campaign (*Collier's*, Sep 28 1946)
What Does She See in Him? (*McCall's*, Sept 1949)
Woods Full of Parsons (*Collier's*, Dec 31 1949)
You Want to Watch a Tourist Every Minute (*Collier's*, Feb 10
    1951)

BACK COUNTRY

WILLIAM FULLER

INTRODUCTION BY
BILL PRONZINI

Black Gat Books • Eureka California

BACK COUNTRY

Published by Black Gat Books
A division of Stark House Press
1315 H Street
Eureka, CA 95501, USA
griffinskye3@sbcglobal.net
www.starkhousepress.com

BACK COUNTRY
Originally published by Dell Publishing Company, Inc., New York, and
copyright © 1954 by William Fuller.

"William Fuller is Brad Dolan" copyright © 2022 by Bill Pronzini

ISBN-13: 978-1-951473-59-4

Cover and text design by Jeff Vorzimmer, ¡caliente!design, Austin, Texas
Proofreading by Bill Kelly

PUBLISHER'S NOTE:
This is a work of fiction. Names, characters, places and incidents are either
the products of the author's imagination or used fictionally, and any
resemblance to actual persons, living or dead, events or locales, is entirely
coincidental.

First Stark House Press/Black Gat Edition: February 2022

William Fuller *is* Brad Dolan
By Bill Pronzini

Who is Brad Dolan?

For readers unfamiliar with the protagonist of *Back Country* and five subsequent 1950s novels, here is a capsule sketch: Hardbitten veteran of two wars, with a checkered past in which he ran guns from Tangiers to Saudi Arabia and smuggled aliens into the Louisiana marshes from Mexico. Former advertising exec embittered by the blatant infidelity of his ex-wife Dusty. Adventurer who resorts to violence and to skirting, bending, or breaking the law when circumstances warrant. Wanderer whose primary ambitions are fishing and "blue water, sunshine, and freedom," his reason for buying and renovating an old commercial fishing boat and cruising the Florida keys and the Caribbean—a forerunner of John D. MacDonald's Travis McGee. Complex individual: reflective, opinionated, compassionate, well-read, and an admirer of classical music. His one admitted weakness: "getting jammed up with women."

In *Back Country*, Dolan is on his way from New York to Miami when his car breaks down in Cartersville, a small rural town between Lake Okeechobee and the Kissimmee River in central Florida. The town, he soon discovers, is a hotbed of gambling, bootleg whiskey, sporting houses, cockfights, and other illegal activities, all of it run by Rand Ringo.

After running afoul of the local law and spending a night in jail, Dolan is summoned to Ringo's home where he's surprised by the offer of a job in the kingpin's Carter County organization. He makes the mistake of accepting the offer in order to build himself a stake—and Ringo makes the mistake of believing this means he owns Dolan. Complications arise when

Dolan becomes involved with his employer's beautiful daughter and equally beautiful alcoholic wife, the racially charged troubles of a Black bonita (numbers) operator, a viciously corrupt sheriff, a martini-swilling madam, and a plot to wrench control of Carter County away from Ringo. Matters come to a head in an explosive climax.

William Fuller's talent for creating vividly believable characters, his fine sense of place, his well-integrated anecdotal material (much of it no doubt autobiographical), and liberal doses of action and sex make *Back Country* a compelling read. (There is some racist language and opinion typical of the prevailing attitudes in the rural South during the Jim Crow era. However, none of the racism is expressed or endorsed by either Brad Dolan or the author.)

The novel was an immediate success when originally published as a Dell First Edition in 1954, selling out its first printing in three months and half a million copies overall. Advance and newspaper reviews were uniformly favorable. Brett Halliday, the creator of Michael Shayne, labeled it "literate, hard-paced violence, remindful of James M. Cain," and went on to state that "Brad Dolan is believably tough, mentally as well as physically." The Long Beach, CA, *Press-Telegram* called the novel the "biggest quarter's worth of suspense on the paperback stands." Other reviews found it to be "exciting, strong and uninhibited", and that it "has traces of *All the King's Men*, Faulkner, and Mickey Spillane."

Who was William Fuller?

To begin with, this is what he had to say about himself in a biographical sketch in a 1949 issue of *Adventure*: "Born [in Roxbury, MA] in 1913. Two years of college. Jobs: deckhand on freighters and tankers in the Atlantic, Pacific and Gulf of Mexico (with intermittent periods of time on the beach in San

Francisco and New Orleans), migratory farm worker, short order cook, Hollywood extra (westerns, mostly), newspaper reporter, various publicity stints (including a six-month tour of duty hauling and herding four models in red wigs—known as the 'Macy Redheads'— around to all the better New York nightspots)."

At the outset of World War II Fuller joined the army, serving as a cavalry officer and as an infantryman on Guam, Leyte, and Okinawa. While still stationed stateside in 1942, he met Eunice Bourne Lee, the granddaughter of the founder of Packard Motors and a budding stage actress who appeared in the Broadway play, *A Kiss for Cinderella*. They were married later that year, and the first of their three sons was born two years later. After Fuller's military stint ended, he and his family settled in Florida and made Winter Haven their permanent home in 1947.

Fuller's writing career was divided into two distinctly different parts. The first was composed entirely of short stories. He made his initial sale to an air-war pulp, *Sky Aces*, in 1940, but it was not until 1945 that he began producing, with remarkable success, a series of stories aimed at the so-called "slick magazines." From 1946 to 1953 he published 26 stories, twenty of which appeared in *Collier's*, two in *McCall's*, and one in *Esquire*. The remaining three were printed in *Adventure* (2) and *Argosy*. Most were sharply drawn character studies of rural Floridians and tales of dogs and other animals. A small number dealt with his experiences in the military and as a Hollywood film extra. None were in the mystery/suspense vein; only one, in fact, "Special Deputy" (*Collier's*, Nov. 8, 1952), has more than marginal criminous content.

Why Fuller decided to abandon the lucrative slick magazine market to write lusty action/adventure novels for the burgeoning paperback field is unknown. It may have been at the suggestion of his agent, or he may have read, admired, and sought to emulate and capitalize on the success of such best-selling Florida-based writers as John D. MacDonald, Charles Williams, Gil Brewer, Day Keene, and Harry Whittington. In any case, he wrote and sold the first two Brad Dolans in 1953-1954, and four more plus one standalone suspense novel over the next five years. All were published as Dell First Editions.

There is evidence to suggest that the second Dolan novel, *Goat Island*, which also appeared in 1954 (and was later reprinted as *Local Talent*), was written prior to *Back Country*. The first 61 pages take place in New York City, and are peopled by violent standard-brand gangsters out to steal $35,000 entrusted to Dolan by a close friend who was later murdered in Florida. When Dolan is severely beaten and the money taken, he vows vengeance and trails the thugs south to a fishing camp on remote Goat Island, one of the Ten Thousand Islands near the Everglades. The novel strengthens once Dolan arrives in Florida, but *Back Country* is a more focused and accomplished work—a fact that may have convinced Dell's editors to bring it out first.

Fuller's third novel, *The Pace that Kills* (1956), is the only one that doesn't feature Dolan. Written third-person and set in the swampland of Oklachoppee County, it tells the violent tale of the hunt for a murderous escapee from Raiford State Prison who terrorizes the region and changes the lives of three men and two women. *The Saturday Review of Literature*, which was not always kind to paperback originals, praised its pacing (with the caveat that "promiscuity abounds") and gave it a plus mark.

The Girl in the Frame (1957), Dolan #3, is arguably the best book in the series. Cruising in his newly acquired boat, *Jessie*, Dolan chances on an unnamed island occupied by a couple named Chalmers living in the ruins of a sugar plantation. A connection between the couple and the disappearance and apparent murder of a judge in the resort town of Key Luna, for which Dolan was framed and nearly killed, is the central plot element in this suspenseful, twist-laden adventure.

Set in Cuba and the fictional Republica de Guajira, *Brad Dolan's Blonde Cargo* (1957) has Dolan mixed up with a Latin femme fatale and banana republic politics. *The Saturday Review* was also kind to this novel, opining: "Seamanship excellent and background pleasant; casualties heavy in Central American dust-up."

In *Brad Dolan's Miami Manhunt* (1958), Dolan encounters a floor-show stripper while on vacation in Miami who talks him into helping her recover a stolen quarter of a million dollars hidden by her dead husband. The search, imperiled by hard cases also after the money, leads from Miami's neon jungle to a deserted island in the Bahamas.

Fuller made a costly error in judgment with his final novel, *Tight Squeeze* (1959). He has Dolan once more involved in a revolution, a genuine one this time—in sympathetic league with the rebels fighting to overthrow the Cuban government by smuggling guns to them on board the *Jessie*. Once the weapons are delivered, he joins the insurgents in a bloody takeover of a town called Santa Clara in order to rescue a woman being held prisoner by "Batista's strongboys."

The controversial pro-Castro theme could not have set well with some readers, given what transpired after the Fidelista takeover; it was likely the reason why the book did not sell as well as the previous Dolans, and why Dell decided to end the series. The decisions, Fuller's and Dell's, may also have been responsible, directly or indirectly, in ending his writing career. For whatever reason he published nothing more after 1959, at least not under his own name.

Most of the last two-plus decades of Fuller's life were spent as owner and operator of a charter-fishing boat. He died in Winter Haven in 1982.

—Petaluma, California
July 2021

BACK COUNTRY

WILLIAM FULLER

Chapter One

I left Highway 41 and headed east for the Gold Coast. The macadam road waved and dipped like a live thing. Canals, shimmering in heat waves, stretched along either side of the road. Egrets stood knee deep in the dirty-brown water of these canals and lumbered into the air from a standing start as they tuned in on the roar of my beat-up Ford. Every few miles I passed the crunched red guts of moccasins that had made the mistake of wondering if the frogs were greener on the other side of the road. Beyond the canals was wasteland—saw grass prairies, palm islands, nothing. An occasional gray cypress stood rooted in slime like a tired G.I. on guard duty.

If this is Florida, I thought, they can have it.

The saw grass prairies gave way to palmetto scrub dotted with lean range cattle. Then the road rocked through barren pine flats. I gunned the Ford. I was somewhere north of Lake Okeechobee, somewhere close to the Kissimmee River valley—and all I wanted of inland Florida was out. Fifty or sixty miles straight east and a little bit south was the Florida I'd heard about and read about and seen pictured in the travel posters—the white beaches, the blue sea, the lazy palms, the women soaking up sunshine in Bikini bathing suits—and the angles.

I passed a sign that said: "WELCOME TO CARTER COUNTY. STAY AWHILE—YOU'LL LIKE IT!" I had to laugh.

That's when the Ford started clattering—bad. It sounded like all hell had broken loose. I jerked to a stop and got out, cussing. I lifted the lid and had a look. I'd thrown a rod. I don't know what I might have expected. I'd had the pedal on the floor for the best part of two days and a night—all the way from Walter Reed, where the Army had turned me loose with a small fortune in silver plate in my left leg and a medical discharge. I had been in a hurry. You lie in a ditch somewhere east of Wonsan in Korea for seventy hours and your leg looks like something laid out on a butcher's block and it's thirty degrees below zero—you can get pretty cold. And you never want to be cold again. For me, it had been a tossup between the desert country in the Southwest and Florida. I had soldiered in the Big One with a guy named Jake McHenry. I had Jake's latest letter in my pocket:

... it's a soft touch, Brad. Think of yourself, boy. You give them five years the first time and two years the second time and in between you're knocking yourself out for peanuts. So what have you got now? You've got a hole in your leg. Get smart, boy. The Man likes 'em big and rough. I've told him about you. This Miami is Angle Town, pal. Easy Money Row. You get your discharge, you come on down ...

That letter had decided me.

I figured I could make civilization if I cooled the Ford out and took it easy. I cranked up and limped and clattered along at a fast fifteen miles an hour. The scenery improved—I'll give it that. I was crossing hammock-land now. Giant live oaks squatted beside the road on either side, and twenty feet above the road their branches met in a dark tangle of leaves and Spanish moss. I started seeing signs plugging business establishments in a town called Cartersville. *Demetrios' Presto Lunch—Fine Old Southern Cuisine.* I'd had these Fine Old Southern Cuisines in jerkwater deep-Southern towns before. Fried chicken stiff with grease, heavy biscuits, a dried-out yam and limp coleslaw. Demetrios could have it. And *The Cartersville Ritz—A Home Away From Home.* I'd had these country Ritzes, too, with their iron bedsteads and their lumpy mattresses and their fifty-watt light bulbs hanging naked from the ceiling from a cord wrapped with flypaper covered with weeks-old flies. Thank you, no.

In ten minutes I was in Cartersville. The town lay sleeping on four sides of a dusty park. I took it twice around the park, just looking. A railroad track ran through the center of the park. On one side of the tracks was a bandstand. On the other, a World War Number I memorial plaque. At one end of the park three or four old men were poking a shuffleboard puck up and down a court and cackling at one another. Under a rubber tree beyond the shuffleboard court a half-dozen men had a red-hot pinochle game going. They slammed the cards on the table the way men with little to do but play pinochle or acey-deucey always do. I would have laid money there was a barber and at least one real estate-insurance man in the game. I drove once more around the park thinking. *This is the Florida the tourists never see,* I thought. *This is small town anywhere.*

The town stank and I wanted none of it—except a good fast mechanic. But for the time it took me to drive two times around that park I got sort of a wheeze out of it. I'd been raised in a town about the size of this one, myself. I wouldn't be caught dead in it now, but I suddenly remembered, for the first time in years, the band concerts in the park on Sundays and on the Fourth of July, and the time we'd planted the alarm clock in old man Elliot's tuba. We'd set the clock so it would go off right in the middle of the concert, and it had gone off right on schedule and loused up "The Stars and Stripes Forever."

And I remembered how we'd tossed the giant firecracker under the pinochle table in our park, and the beating my old man had given me for that one. And how when J. P. Withers had died, his widow had asked Gum Jethroe, the druggist, to prepare J. P.'s stomach properly and send it to the State laboratory to have it checked for malignant growth. And how Gum had left

J.P.'s stomach on the table in his back room for a minute while he went out front and sold a customer a box of Carter's Little Liver Pills, and how Gum's cat had jumped onto the table, latched onto J.P.'s stomach, and taken off down the alley with it. I started thinking about things like that, and how I'd take my girl to the movies on Saturday nights, and then down to Gum's for a chocolate ice cream soda with the gang, and how happy and peaceful it had all been, and ...

For the birds, for God's sake, I thought.

Here I was—getting soft about some lousy hick town. Like I said, all I wanted was a good fast mechanic.

I pulled into a seedy-looking garage. A tall, lean, sad-faced cracker wiped his hands on a batch of waste and listened to my story. He grunted and poked beneath the lid.

"Uh huh," he said.

"How long?"

He took his time answering me. "Tomorrow, maybe. Maybe the day after tomorrow. If I can find the time."

"Do it tonight," I said. "I'll pay your overtime." He looked at a point about ten yards beyond me, his eyes narrowed.

"You ain't working for Mr. Ringo, by any chance?"

"Who in hell is Mr. Ringo?"

He turned to his bench. "Tomorrow," he said. "If I can find the time."

And so I ended up parking my bag beside an iron bedstead under a fifty-watt light bulb in Cartersville's Home Away From Home.

I had a quick bath and a change of clothes and went down to the lobby. My leg was stiff from driving. It was five o'clock in the afternoon and I wanted a drink. I went to the desk.

"Where's the bar?"

The desk clerk delicately removed a stove match from between brown teeth. I've seen friendlier eyes on a dead mackerel.

"Dry county, mister."

I'd hit them before, of course, but I'd thought Florida was different. "All right," I said. "So it's dry. Where can I get a bottle?"

He stared at me with those dead eyes. "You acquainted with Mr. Rand Ringo?"

"No," I said.

"Package store over the county line. That's thirty miles."

"Nice progressive section you've got here," I said.

"Suits us." He put the stove match back in his teeth.

All right. So I wouldn't have a drink before chow. I wandered through town. There wasn't much to it. A yellow brick county courthouse squatted morosely on one corner. I saw a Baptist church and a Methodist church. They didn't look very prosperous. There were three rambling, tin-roofed vegetable warehouses and packing-houses, and a number of tractor and farm implement establishments. There were the usual knots of loafers—white and colored—around the steps of the courthouse and the loading platforms of the packinghouses. The white men stuck together and so did the Negroes. The men squatted or leaned, staring at nothing, or shuffled their feet, stared at the ground, and talked in low voices. I had almost forgotten what it was like in a country town. But there was something different here. I couldn't put my finger on it—but I felt it. And the difference was a thing I'd seen somewhere, sometime, before.

I went to Demetrios'. The lights glared from the ceiling, the way they do in all cheap restaurants. I thought too much of my stomach to go for Demetrios' Fine Old Southern Cuisine. I ordered shrimp cocktail and a sirloin steak. I'm a pretty big man. It takes calories to keep me going. The waitress was thin and looked overworked. I tried to get a smile out of her, but she wouldn't give. The shrimps were all right and the steak was edible. Three men were eating at the table next to mine. They were talking. I couldn't help listening.

"Know that ten thousand acres of Charley Mason's? That rangeland by the river?"

"Yeah."

"Heard he lost it today."

"Yeah?"

"Who you reckon took title to that property?"

"I could guess."

"Well, you guessed it right. Ringo."

I finished my coffee, took my check, and went to the cashier's counter. A fat Greek—Demetrios himself, I supposed—was nursing a cigar behind his cash register. I paid my bill. The constant references to a man named Ringo were beginning to get on my nerves. First the mechanic. Then the desk clerk. Then these three men. I wondered how one man could be that important to a community.

I said, loud enough for the three men behind me to hear, "What's so important about a man named Ringo?"

Demetrios' face blanched. The men behind me were silent.

Demetrios swallowed. "You have good dinner?"

"I've had worse. What about Ringo?"

"You just passing through, mister?"

"Yes."

"Good," Demetrios said. He rang up my cash, shoved my change at me. "That's real good, you're just passing through."

I grinned at him and left.

The thought of spending an evening in Cartersville's Home Away From Home sickened me. I walked around the square. There was one moldy-looking theater in town. I'd seen the movie playing there more than a year before, in Tokyo. I'd never seen a town yet that didn't have a little night life somewhere—if you could find it. Anything would beat that fifty-watt light bulb. I crossed the square to a taxi stand. A cabby dozed in the front seat of a battered 1941 Plymouth. I shook him awake.

"I'm just passing through and I don't know Rand Ringo," I said.

The cabby stared slack-jawed at me as if I were crazy.

"We'll start from there. I'm restless. There must be a couple of places in this county where a man can have a couple of drinks and a few laughs. How about it?"

"Well, we got a juke or so. Outside of town."

I climbed into the front seat with him. "Crank this heap," I said.

"These jukes, they're a ways out of town. They'll cost you—"

"Crank it up, pal," I said.

Joe's Place was eight miles out of town beside a crumbling asphalt county road. The light from the front door picked out a greasy pool on the shell driveway. Hillbilly juke noises rasped and wailed. The cabby stayed with his Plymouth. I went inside. The joint looked like ten thousand other deep-Southern jukes. There was the sign behind the beer counter about credit making enemies so let's stay friends. The Jax beer ads. The juke with the swirling colors. The corn meal on the warped and splintery floor. The shadowy booths sheltering couples who wanted to make their pitch in the dark. The stale and musty smell ...

When I had given my cabby a ten spot he'd warmed up enough to tell me the fun went on in an outbuilding behind the juke. I was to tell the fat man behind the beer bar that Al said I was okay. The fat man was leaning against his bar. I walked across the room toward him, but he didn't look up. He was watching a horsefly move jerkily through the beer-stickiness on the surface of his bar. I saw him tense, then slap a leather poker dice cup against the bar where the horsefly had been. The fly buzzed away.

"Goddamn that fly!" he said. He looked up. "Something?"

"Bottle of Jax."

He reached into his cooler for it. "I'll get that goddamn fly yet."

"With that dice cup? The hard way, isn't it?"

"I figure I'm giving him a sporting chance. Why, I don't know. Except it gives a guy something to do. He'll be back. Then I'll get him."

The juke was pounding away. A drawling, nasal, Texas voice was singing that he was long gone, long gone 'cause some woman from El Paso'd made a traveler out of him.

A couple of country kids had come out of the gloom of one of the booths and were solemnly stiff-legging it around the dance floor, sawing their arms up and down.

I saw the horsefly zoom in for a three-point landing at the far end of the bar. The fat man went tense again. "A buck says you're wrong," I said.

The fat man's eyes were on the fly. From the corner of his mouth he said, "Even money?"

"Even money."

"You're on."

The fly minced down the bar, lifting his legs high, trying to shake the stickiness from his feet. The fat man's jowls purpled as he held his breath. He slapped the dice cup onto the bar. The fly buzzed away, circled, and came back.

The fat man cursed.

"You got to be loose," I said. "You're all tensed up. Here, let me show you."

He handed me the dice cup.

"Same bet?"

"Same bet."

I lifted the bottle of beer to my mouth with one hand and slapped the dice cup onto the bar with the other. I set the empty Jax bottle on the bar then, slid the dice cup to the edge of the counter, cupped my free hand under it, and held the cup with both hands to the fat man's ear. The fly buzzed frantically inside the cup.

I grinned. "You want him?"

"Let the sonofabitch go. He'll be back. Then *I'll* get him."

"You got to be loose, pal."

The fat man turned, rang up a *No Sale* on his register, scooped two dollar bills from the drawer, and tossed them to the bar.

"All right, Sporting Life," he said.

"Forget it, pal. You buy me the beer. I just wanted to see if I was lucky tonight."

He narrowed fat-rimmed eyes at me. "Meaning what?"

"Al knows I'm okay. The cab driver. He's out front taking a nap."

"Al, huh?" He kept staring at me. Then his eyes strayed to the two singles on the bar. "Well, I reckon you're all right. If you ain't I'll have my ass in a buzz saw." I saw his fat hand stray to a buzzer beneath his bar. "Straight back and knock on the door."

I started for the back door. When I got there I looked round. The fat man was staring at his bar again, the poker dice cup in his hand. His whole body was tensed and his jowls were turning purple again. I grinned. *Some guys*, I thought, *will never learn*. But at least I'd met a man who hadn't mentioned Rand Ringo.

A colored man answered my knock at the door of the one-story frame building a hundred yards behind the juke. He bowed me into a brilliantly lighted room. The house was getting a real good play. Men bellied shoulder-to-shoulder to the crap table on one side of the room. A half-dozen quarter and fifty-cent slot machines were being fed coins as fast as they would take them. There were two tables of poker and three of blackjack.

At the rear of the building were two small rooms. One was an office. The top three-quarters of the wall between the main room and the office had been knocked away. A thin, ferret-faced character—the boss, I figured—was standing in his office leaning over the sawed-off wall. He was watching me pretty closely. When I looked at him he shifted his eyes. I could see a bar through the open door of the other room. A colored man in a white jacket was tending it. I headed for it, ordered a double Old Forester and water and went back into the main room. Something pretty exciting seemed to be going on at the crap table. Somebody having a hot run, I supposed.

I went to the table and shouldered my way to a spot at the rim. Directly across the table from me I saw what was causing the excitement—and as far as I was concerned it had nothing to do with hot runs or cold runs. The blonde standing there was exciting enough. Her shining hair was pulled straight back from her forehead and caught in the back with a scrap of ribbon. Her eyes were huge, and a deep, almost violet, blue. She'd been around, this girl—it was there in the set of her mouth. She was thirty, perhaps, or a well-lived twenty-seven. She was beautifully tanned. One shoulder strap of her sheer dress had slipped its moorings, and there was a line across her full, high breast where the tan left off and the milky whiteness began. It was not until she moved, stiffly, mechanically, to place her bet—ten blue chips, a hundred bucks—on the line that I noticed that she was quite drunk.

"New point coming out," the stick man droned.

The bets went down around the table. The blonde was the shooter. She selected two dice from the dozen the stick man offered her. She rolled them down the table. They hit the rim, spun, and died with the two and the one showing.

The stick man sang, "Crap, a loser! Winner in the field."

"Jesus, she's cold," I heard someone whisper. "That must be two thousand she's blown!"

The girl shoved the rest of her chips—eight or ten—onto the line. She handled the dice and threw them, her face expressionless. They bounced off the rim and stopped spinning.

"Caught a nine," the stick man chanted.

The girl threw them hard. She rolled a five and then an eight and on the third roll the two showed immediately and the other die spun crazily for a moment, then rolled to a standstill with the five up. I watched the girl. She sat there, her eyes wide, her lips slightly parted, as her chips were scooped away and the dice went to the next player.

"A new shooter, and a good one!"

The blonde must have felt my stare. She looked at me. There were little shining lights in those great eyes. She licked her lips.

I cashed a twenty and threw a few bucks into the game as the dice made their rounds. I played the Big Six and the Big Eight, just feeling the game out, testing my luck, and my luck was good. By the time the dice reached me I had picked up thirty or forty bucks.

I dropped four yellow chips—twenty dollars—on the line and picked two dice from those scattered before me. The stick man said, "Coming out for a new point," and I threw them down the table. I had a feeling they were going to be real good, and they were—a five and a six. I let the forty ride, blew on the dice, and threw them hard.

"Seven—a front-line winner!"

I knew I should have dragged, but the blonde was staring at me and I felt hot. I let the eighty ride. The dice showed a ten, and I sweated them out for seven or eight rolls before I made my ten the hard way with the five and the five. People were beginning to pay a little attention to me. This was a country crap game and most of the bets—other than the blonde's—were, I noticed, for singles and fins. I'd had three passes in a row. I didn't feel too good about the next one; I had a hunch it might be sour. I dragged a hundred and fifty of the one-sixty—and crapped out with snake eyes. I rolled the dice in my hand, feeling them, and they felt good again, and I slapped the hundred and fifty I'd palmed to the line.

"New point coming out!"

I threw them.

"Caught a five," the stick man chanted.

The dice came back to me and I let them go, hard, then stood grinning at the two and the three.

I guess it didn't make sense to push my luck. But I did. I let the three hundred ride.

"Coming out for a new point!"

"One more time, you sweethearts," I whispered. The six showed first and I knew that when the other die stopped spinning it would be either a five or a one. I knew it just as I knew my name was Brad Dolan. Just as I knew I'd pushed my luck far enough. "Eleven—a winner!"

I pocketed five hundred and ninety-five dollars worth of chips, left a single yellow chip on the line, threw a four, and sevened out two throws later. I grinned at the blonde. She stared at me, her face expressionless. I turned and left the crap table. I was pretty sure she'd follow me. I traded my chips for six hundred and twenty bucks at the cashier's window and went to the bar.

Without looking up I could tell when the girl was standing beside me. I could smell her. She smelled good—good and expensive. I turned to her. She was a tall girl, a big girl. I'm well over six feet myself and she wasn't many inches shorter. I knew this girl was not local talent. They don't smell that expensive, they don't wear their dresses that well, they don't even tan that well when they come from country towns like Cartersville. I would have laid even money that she had put in time somewhere as either a model or a showgirl. She had the body for it and the face for it.

"Well, hello," I said.

Her voice was a little thick. "Why did you quit?"

I grinned. "You quit when you're ahead."

"You were hot. You were chicken to quit."

"I've got money in my pocket." Maybe I shouldn't have rubbed it in. "You?"

"There's plenty where mine came from!"

"Oh?"

"As much as I want!"

It sounded as if she were trying to defend herself, trying to justify her position, whatever it was. I looked at her. She was staring at me with those wide-open eyes. All of a sudden it dawned upon me that this girl was badly frightened. Whoever supplied the money she had been spending was pretty obviously going to give her a bad time for losing it. I'd seen that wide-eyed stare, that set, expressionless face, on G.I.'s in shock. There's nothing as humiliating, as degrading, as fear. Two wars had taught me that. I felt a sudden, harsh resentment against anyone who made other people afraid. *Wait a minute, Dolan*, I told myself. *Cool out. You're not fighting wars any more. You're out looking for laughs—remember? So stop making like a Boy Scout.*

I took a deep breath. It made me feel calmer. "It's nice to know rich girls. Let me buy you a drink, rich girl."

She was still staring at me. She nodded.

I turned to the bartender. "Give the lady what she's been drinking. Make mine Old Forester and water. And—"

"No more for the lady," a voice behind me said.

"Yes, sir, Mr. Fanchon," the bartender said.

I spun on my heels. There was the ferret-faced man I'd seen in the office.

"What do you mean, no more for the lady?" I said.

The girl stared at him. "Damn you, Joe!"

"You've had enough, Billy."

"I'm buying her a drink," I said.

I looked over Joe's shoulder. A couple of fairly tough looking characters—bouncers, by the looks of them—were on their way.

"Go home, Billy," Joe said.

"No!" Billy said.

"You heard the lady, pal," I said. "That's your clue. Blow!"

"Listen, mister," Joe said. "We don't want no trouble. Why don't you just hit the road, huh? Come on, now. Outside!"

There are ways of saying and doing things. I lost my temper. Joe wasn't big enough to hit, really. So I grabbed the lapels of his coat with my left hand and lifted him off his feet and slapped him two or three times—not too hard. Then I dropped him. One of the bouncers charged me. Billy screamed. I braced my back against the bar and let this party have a hard knee in his belly. He grunted once as the wind left him and he went to the floor on all fours and stayed there gasping for breath. I had used my left knee on him—the left leg was the one with the new silver in it—and it hurt like hell.

Billy screamed, "Look out!"

The other guy was coming at me swinging a sap. I ducked and came up swinging wildly and I felt my left fist crunch against jawbone. He grunted and staggered a little, then shook his head and came back in again swinging that sap. I side-stepped him and clipped him with a right cross to the side of his head as he went by. The one on the floor was grappling for my knees now

and I half fell, off balance, back against the bar. I had
been awfully dumb. I had forgotten about Joe. I heard
Billy scream again and that's the last thing I heard for
awhile. Just as she screamed I felt something bite into
the back of my skull and I tasted every filling in my
teeth and then I felt the floor come up and hit me.

I was crawling through wet jungle on my hands and
knees. I was tired. I could hardly lift my hands and my
knees from the clinging jungle mud but I knew I had to
do it. A Jap platoon was bivouacked in three nipa huts
in a clearing just ahead. I had the B.A.R. and in a very
few minutes I could stand and move into those nipa
huts firing the B.A.R. from the hip and raking the huts
at floor level for the sleeping ones, and slightly above
floor level for the sitting ones, and then a little higher
for the standing ones—and then none of them would
be left. But the crawling was hard. Wet bushes kept
slapping me in the face. My head was aching and every
time a wet bush would slap me my head would throb
worse than ever.

"Wake up, bum!"

I opened my eyes. I was lying on a wooden bench.
A big, bullet-headed man with eyes like an angry pig
was standing over me. He had a wet towel in one hand.
"Wake up, bum," he said again. He swung the towel
and it slapped me across the face, hard. Then I sat up.
When the room stopped spinning I knew where I was.

I was in a room in a back-country county
courthouse. I knew it was a back-country county
courthouse. They're all alike. They smell alike. They
smell of musty, dusty records and sweat and bad
plumbing and dirty spittoons and floors that need
scrubbing and staleness and time that hangs heavy and
chicken-little deals that are made around the corner. I
looked around the room. Two men leaned back in
chairs across the room and smirked at me. They were
big, red-faced, pot-gutted men—almost as big and red-

faced and pot-gutted as the man with the wet towel. A
sign on the desk across the room said *Sheriff Loy
Bailey*.

"Tell me this," I said. "Why is it all you country
sheriffs and deputies run to fat?"

He slapped me across the face with his towel.

"Maybe you spend too much time on your tails,
boys. You ought to get off your tails. You ought to get
a little exercise."

He slapped me again. My head throbbed.

"You're a big, brave man—ain't you, bum?" he
said.

"Must be a frostie, Loy," one of the deputies said.
"All these snowbirds is full of piss and vinegar when
they first get down here to God's country."

The other deputy slapped his thigh and guffawed.

The sheriff clamped yellowed teeth to the butt-end
of a plug of Brown's Mule and wrenched a chew away.
He tucked it in his jaw. "We got enough on this here
frostie to thaw him out for a spell," Loy said. "Assault
and battery. Wilful destruction of property. Drunk and
disorderly. I reckon the county solicitor can figure out
a few more charges."

I remembered then to slap my hip pocket to see if
my wallet was there. I should have known better. It
was gone, of course. In addition to the cash I'd picked
up at Joe Fanchon's crap table that evening I'd had just
under two hundred dollars of my own. Plus my driver's
license, the photostat of my Army discharge and the
other odds and ends that a man usually carries in his
wallet. I had a couple of grand in a bank in
Washington, so I wasn't exactly broke. But I couldn't
afford to blow some eight hundred bucks, either.

The sheriff slapped me again with his wet towel. I
gripped the edge of the bench until my knuckles turned
white to keep from coming off that bench at him. I
knew I wouldn't stand a chance. I'd been hurt enough
for one night.

"On your feet, bum," Loy growled.

I staggered to my feet. The three of them herded me through the door, down the hall, past an alcove with a dusty figure of Justice balancing her scales in it, down the front steps, and into the back seat of a car. One of the deputies squeezed his pot-gut under the wheel. Loy Bailey labored in beside him and the other deputy hunched beside me in the back. We drove down the main drag. There were still a few people on the sidewalks. They just seemed to stand there, staring at nothing, and I had that feeling I'd had earlier in the evening that there was something about this town that was different from other country towns. Something that I had seen somewhere, sometime, before. Something I didn't like.

We stopped in front of a two-story red brick building—the county jail. The three men herded me up the steps and through the main room to the single cell block in the rear. An old man with a sad and broken face was asleep, his head back, snoring, in a chair by the cell block door. Loy Bailey shook him awake. "Goddamn, you sleep messy," he said. "On your feet, you old fart. Fresh meat."

The old man flashed a look of pure hatred at him, creaked to his feet and fumbled open the cell block door. He led the way to an empty cell, and Bailey and his deputies escorted me to it. Bailey led me in. He turned to go, then wheeled—very fast for a man his size—and threw a hamlike fist at my face. I caught it on my left cheek and went down on the dirty cement floor.

"There ain't but one kind of exercise I like, bum," he said. "That's it." Then the Sheriff of Carter County kicked me in the ribs, and I didn't have what it took to get off the floor. He spat a stream of tobacco juice at my legs.

"Always did ease my nerves to see tobacco juice running off a man's legs," he said.

The other deputies guffawed at this rare bit of rural wit. I caught a glimpse of the old jailer; he was trembling, and his face looked sick with disgust. Bailey slammed the cell door shut and they all left me alone. I crawled to the lower bunk and pulled myself up on the dirty, stinking mattress. I knew now what the difference was between this town and other country towns I'd seen and lived in, and I knew now where and when I'd seen it. I'd spent the tag end of World War Two in a German prison camp. In Stalag Number XI we had all been weary, beaten. There had been a general attitude of why the hell fight back. We had shuffled through our chores and we had stared at nothing. There had been little laughter. The Cartersville that I had seen was like that.

Chapter Two

I came awake the next morning to the sight of a king-sized cockroach crawling over the dish of cold oatmeal somebody had brought me for breakfast. I was feeling pretty rocky but I guessed I'd live. I winced as I felt the cut on my head where Joe Fanchon—I supposed it had been Joe—had sapped me. It was plenty tender, but it seemed to have healed clean. My left jaw was a little creaky and my ribs were sore from the sheriff's use of his subtle powers of persuasion— but I didn't think there was anything wrong with me that a hot bath, a shave, and a good breakfast wouldn't cure.

Physically, then, I was on the mend. Mentally I was all fouled up. Once more I had gotten myself in a jam over some broad. It was a weakness of mine. If I hadn't gotten hungry for that full, ripe body and that tanned skin, I would be waking up now in Cartersville's Home Away From Home. But here I was in a stinking, dirty jail, in a stinking, dirty town with no money, no identification, no friends, no nothing. God only knew what sort of charges they'd booked me on. I held my head in my hands and groaned.

I closed my eyes and tried to make a plan and all I could see were those big blue eyes of Billy's, with the fear in them, and I couldn't concentrate on anything else. I wondered if those months in the hospital had made me soft. Maybe Billy had been a part of the setup and I'd been too stupid to see it. Maybe that's the way they treated all the non-regular customers who picked up a few bucks at their lousy crap game. A guy comes in cold, picks up a few bucks, decides to quit while he's ahead, and Billy gives him the business. The guy goes for her, naturally, and that's Joe's cue to start talking rough. With Billy there the sucker feels feisty enough to talk back, and it ends up in a roughhouse with the guy getting himself sapped, then slapped around by Loy Bailey and his deputies, and waking up with no wallet.

Maybe that's the way it was. Somehow, though, I just couldn't buy it.

"Mr. Dolan?"

I looked up, surprised. The old jailer was rattling a key in the lock on my cell door. The door swung open. I just sat there on my bunk.

"You're Mr. Dolan, ain't you?"

"That's right."

Now the old man sounded petulant. "Well, come on. I ain't got time to stand here all day talking."

"Cool out, pop," I said. "Where're we going?"

"Me, I ain't going nowhere. I'll tell you the truth, mister, the way I work around here tending to this jailhouse, why I'd sooner be behind the bars than in front of them. If I was on your side of the bars I wouldn't have a thing in this world to do but set on my ass. On my side of the bars I got to work it to a frazzle. Where you're going is none of my business. All I know is I've been told to turn you a'loose."

I was on my feet. "I'm not being charged with anything?"

"I tell you what do, son. You don't like being turned a'loose then you set right here in this cell and maybe somebody'll change their mind and decide to keep you here."

I grinned at him. "So long, pop." I said.

"Oh," the old man said. "I like to have forgot the most important thing. Mr. Rand Ringo left word that he wants to see you this morning."

I was halfway to the open door of the cell block. I stopped and turned. "Do me a favor, will you, pop?"

"Maybe. Then again maybe not."

"Give Ringo a message. Tell him Mr. Dolan said to stuff it."

The old man's mouth gaped open and then his face lighted with an expression of pure, unadulterated admiration. I turned and left him.

I felt a lot better after a bath and a change of clothes. As I passed the desk on my way to find breakfast the desk clerk stopped me. It was the same desk clerk who'd been on duty when I'd checked in. This time he didn't have a stove match in his teeth and this time he was smiling. "Mr. Dolan," he said, "Mr. Ringo called. Mr. Rand Ringo. He asked me to remind you of your appointment with him this morning."

"I—"

"You know where he lives?"

I shook my head. A man can take just so much. I listened to the desk clerk tell me how to get to Ringo's house in the country. I didn't commit myself one way or the other. When he'd finished talking I asked him if he'd had a call about my car.

"It's outside, sir. Ready to go."

"You pay for it?" I asked, wondering if he'd squawk when I had to write him a check.

"Oh, that's all been taken care of." He waved an airy hand. "Mr. Ringo—"

That did it. I knew I wouldn't have a night's sleep until I met Ringo. I had breakfast at a diner down the street. Then I started for Ringo's house. I was in no hurry. I had time to kill. I had a little unfinished business at Joe's Place. I wanted my wallet back and I had a pretty good idea it was there. I believed I knew how to get it back and I had decided to wait until night because I was hoping that a blonde named Billy would be there to see me get it.

I went out of town the way the desk clerk had told me to go. I drove six miles on a county road, then swung onto a graveled road that was lined on either side with great green banyan trees whose branches met above the road and formed a leafy arch. Beyond the banyans were white fences enclosing beautifully cultivated pasture land that stretched green and shimmering as far as I could see. Fat, sleek Brahman steers fed in the belly-deep grass.

It was a setup. If all this was Ringo's, then Ringo must be rolling rich. Even with this kind of preparation Ringo's house took me by surprise. The graveled road swung sharply to the right and the arch of banyans ended and there it was—a huge, expensive, sprawling, bewildering hulk of pink stucco and red-tiled roof, with vine-choked walls and casements and wrought-iron balconies in unlikely spots, and patios that seemed to have been added as an afterthought. It was Spanish, Moorish, Italian, a little bit Georgian with Colonial overtones, and somehow, all in all, feudal. It was Florida boom time. It was the Talmadge sisters' and Valentino's Hollywood.

The wide lawn, dark green and velvety, and studded with great live oaks and more banyans, stretched away to the black and winding river that was, I supposed, the Kissimmee. A boathouse big enough to house a family of six squatted at the river's edge. A sleek mahogany speedboat lay at the dock by the boathouse. Five hundred yards behind the house were white-washed stables. Just beyond my car was a kidney-shaped swimming pool, complete with dressing-rooms, deck chairs, rubber mattresses, and all the works.

I left my Ford, walked to the brass-studded front door and rang the bell. The door swung open almost immediately. A white-wooled old colored man grinned at me.

"Mr. Dolan, sir?"

"Yes."

"Mr. Ringo, he's waiting for you." He bowed me inside and led me down a high, dark hall. I glanced quickly into a couple of the rooms off the hall and got the impression of heaviness; everything looked dark, cool, old. The old man was knocking at a door now. From inside the room I could hear Mozart's *Concerto in D Minor*, and I hadn't heard that in years.

A smooth voice, deep, cultivated, said, "Come in, please."

The old man opened the door. I glanced quickly around the room. It seemed to be a combination study and office. Shelves of books. Filing cabinets. A record cabinet that stretched the length of one wall, and of course the phonograph. Good, conservative pictures on the walls—watercolors for the most part, and a number of etchings.

Ringo stood at his desk. He was a tall man—as tall as I—but running slightly to flesh around the middle. He was, I guessed, in his late forties. He wore a white shirt, beautifully tailored riding-breeches and glistening, dark brown, soft-leathered riding-boots. His face, neck, wrists, and hands were deeply tanned. His hair was black shot with gray. His jaw was strong, his lips full but firm. These features were all dominated, however, by his eyes; they were huge, soft, luminous, black-brown, with an almost Oriental slant. On a woman they would have been beautiful. On Ringo they seemed as much at variance with the rest of his features as this great, sprawling, castle-like home was at variance with the rural drabness of the Carter County I had seen.

He stood there, waiting. I wouldn't give him the satisfaction of moving toward him. He'd asked to see me. Let him make the first move. I remained where I was, at the door. The colored man beside me coughed nervously. I waited. Ringo waited. Then his full lips twisted in what was obviously intended to be a grin. He moved toward me, his hand outstretched.

"That'll be all, Ben," he said.

Ben sounded relieved. "Yes, sir, Mr. Ringo."

I shook Ringo's hand.

"Thanks for coming, Dolan. Drink?"

"Whatever you're having, Ringo." If he could dispense with the "Mr." then so could I. His face went momentarily hard as he glanced at me. Then he laughed. He started for the portable bar in the corner of his room. "I think you'll do, Dolan," he said.

I didn't want to seem curious. I let it go. I wandered over to the shelves of books and glanced at the titles. He had a good library, if you liked the sort of things he had. It ran heavily to philosophy—from Plato to Santayana—and to psychology—Freud, Jung, Adler, and the others. I took down, at random, Nietzsche's *Thus Spake Zarathustra*. I thumbed through it. It had been well-read by someone. Ringo had moved quickly, noiselessly, beside me.

"You're familiar with that?"

"I've been exposed to it."

"Approve of his theories?" he asked.

"The Superman stuff? The Master Race crap? If I believed in that then I've spent a lot of time fighting for the wrong side," I said.

He laughed again, then handed me a glass of bourbon over ice. I tasted it. It was smooth, mellow, powerful. "You apparently haven't spent much time in the deep South," he said.

"Some," I said.

"If you stay down here awhile you'll change your opinions, Dolan. These people down here are pretty inferior. I'm speaking of the blacks and the whites— the cracker class of whites, that is—alike. Generations of slavery, either actual or economic, have left them incapable of directing their own affairs. They need strength to guide them, Dolan. If certain individuals don't accept the responsibility, the government will have to do it. And there you have socialism—"

"Certain individuals—like yourself, Ringo?"

The luminosity in his eyes was now more of a glitter. "Like myself," he said.

"Who delegates this responsibility?"

I watched his hand clench into a powerful-looking fist. "It's a question of strength, Dolan. The responsibility belongs to the strongest!"

I felt a little sorry for the other people. But I didn't say so.

Ringo got off his soap box. The Mozart was coming to its end. "Like that?" he asked.

"I like anything of Mozart's. But I don't especially prefer the *Concerto in D Minor*."

He snapped it off. "You're quite a man, Dolan. You come busting into Cartersville like a bum on the lam and yet you can talk a little Nietzsche and you know something about Mozart."

"I've been around," I said.

"Where, for instance?"

I gave him a brief resume of the past ten or twelve years, and then was sorry I'd done it. I had that dirty taste in the back of my mouth that I always have when I've done too much talking and not enough listening. I'd even managed, I suspected, to work in a good deal of the bitterness I'd accumulated in the years between the Big One and Korea—in Korea and then, later, in the hospitals. I know I mentioned the fact that my plans for the future were somewhat vague and depended upon where and how I could latch onto some of the things I felt I had coming. I hadn't talked so much about myself in years. And it suddenly dawned upon me that this man Ringo was *making* me talk. He was dominating this conversation, or this near-monologue, just as he dominated the room in which he stood. And I didn't like being dominated.

"All right," I said. "That's too much of that. What did you—"

He interrupted me. "Oh, by the way—" He went to his desk, opened a drawer, and tossed me my wallet.

I caught it and stared at it, stupidly.

"I like the way you handled yourself in Joe Fanchon's place last night, Dolan," he said, "even if the whole thing was rather useless."

I waited.

"I like the way you stood up to Loy Bailey and his deputies—even if that was rather futile also."

"How do you know these things? How did you get my wallet?"

"I know everything that happens in Carter County."

"How?"

The luminosity in his eyes was a glitter again, cruel, ruthless. He hammered a fist into an open palm. "Because, by God, Carter County is mine!"

"Including Joe's Place? Including the sheriff?"

He calmed somewhat. "It's all mine, Dolan. Lock, stock, and barrel. What I don't own, I control."

I stood up. My head throbbed where Ringo's man Joe Fanchon had sapped me. My cheek burned where Ringo's sheriff had thrown a hamlike fist at it. The air was dirty in that room.

"How would you like to work for me, Dolan?"

I didn't have a chance to answer him. The door opened. The girl standing there was nineteen—twenty, at the most. Her face was a delicate oval, her hair was a dark and shining mass, and her skin was a transparent, translucent, off-white cream color. She was dressed in white shorts and a white halter top that left her shoulders bare. Her full breasts were high and thrusting. Her narrow waist flared into softly molded hips and her legs were long and tanned and rounded. Her black-brown eyes were huge and shining, and slanted in an almost Oriental way—and I knew of course that she was Ringo's daughter. I had thought that Ringo's eyes would be beautiful on a woman. I hadn't known how beautiful. I stood there staring at her, and I knew that I had never wanted a woman as much as I wanted this one.

Ringo's voice was soft behind me. "My daughter, Gloria," he said. "Gloria, this is Brad Dolan."

She stared solemnly at me, her face expressionless. When she spoke it was in a husky monotone: "How do you do?"

I nodded.

She went to her father. Her posture, her slowly undulating walk, had a Polynesian grace and fluidity. She stopped beside Ringo, and he leaned forward and kissed her cheek. His hand stroked the shining mass of hair, softly, over and over. Gloria turned to me, slowly. Her face was still expressionless. It was almost as if she were in a trance. There was warmth, there was passion, behind those eyes, those full lips—there had to be. But they were locked away, frozen. I had a sudden desire to shout, to throw something—even to slap this girl. Anything to put expression into that lovely face. I wanted to see her laugh, or cry, or wince with pain— anything.

Ringo's fingers ran lightly down her cheek to her slim neck. "We're talking business, kitten," he said softly. "Run along now. I'll see you at luncheon."

She nodded gravely at him, stared at me for a moment, then moved in her graceful way to the door. I glanced at Ringo. His eyes were following her and they were soft again.

When Gloria had closed the door he turned to me. "About that job," he said. "I need someone like you. You've seen what I have to work with. Joe Fanchon. Loy Bailey. No imagination, no subtlety. They're trash, Dolan. They're loyal, they mean well, but they're trash. You saw them in operation last night. And there are others just as bad—"

"I'm not interested, Ringo," I said. But as I said it I knew it didn't ring true. Not a hundred per cent true. Who was I kidding? No one but myself. I was a guy with no job. I was a guy on the make for some of the things he thought he had coming. And I wasn't too particular how I got them. That's what I'd decided, wasn't it? So where did I get off turning down a thing that might be good? What was there about this particular setup that turned my stomach? And since when had I developed a queasy gut?

"I *need* you, Dolan. Or someone like you. I've been looking for a man like you simply to take over some of the messy details, to be on hand when he's needed. When I heard the way you operated last night I thought you might do. Now that I've talked with you and seen you, I'm sure of it. I need know-how and intelligence and guts in this organization. You told me yourself— not fifteen minutes ago—that you were sick of being shoved around. That you wanted to make up for lost time and that you weren't particularly concerned about how you did it. Isn't that true?"

"Within certain limits," I said.

"I'll make it worth your while, Dolan."

I played for time. "I've talked too much here today, Ringo," I said. "But you've done a good deal of talking, too. You've told me a few things here this morning that I'm sure you wouldn't want repeated. You don't know me, Ringo. I could be a Fed, I could be almost anything, and you've—"

He smiled. "Other than the things you told me about yourself a while ago, Dolan—which, by the way,

I know are all true—here's the rest of the picture." He took a notebook from his hip pocket, thumbed through it for a moment, then put it back in his pocket.

"All right, Dolan," he went on, "you're thirty-one years old. Right?" I said nothing. He smiled. "You were born in a two-bit town called Amasa, in West Virginia. When you finished high school you spent approximately a year and a half in the Merchant Marine, then jumped ship in Tangiers. You were picked up several months later by British authorities and implicated in a gun-running operation between there and Saudi Arabia. You beat that rap—probably because of your tender years—but you were sent home. How am I doing, Dolan?"

I said nothing.

"Quite a kid." He shook his head in mock admiration. "I lose track of you for two years or so here. But then you show up in Mexico City. I haven't any proof of this—but it is rumored that you were contact man for a group of Mexicans who were in the highly profitable business of flying aliens into landing fields behind the coastal marshes of Louisiana. For some undisclosed reason—which might have to do with the leader of your group being found in a back alley with a hole in his head—you left Mexico City in a hurry. It is also rumored that it is not safe for you to go back there."

He grinned at me. "How am I doing, Dolan?" he repeated.

I waited, tensed.

"Maybe you're beginning to understand why I think you'll be valuable to me, Dolan. All right. You enlisted in the infantry in 1941. You were in the fighting on Guadalcanal. You won a Silver Star for gallantry in action there and you were subsequently evacuated stateside with a hole in your chest from a Jap hand grenade. They patched you up and you eventually made the big drop into Normandy with the

101st Airborne. You were given a battlefield commission soon after this. During the defense of Bastogne by the 101st your platoon was cut off and slashed to pieces. Those of you left alive were taken prisoner by the Germans."

He took the notebook from his pocket again. He thumbed through it. "Let's see. Oh, here. I lose you for almost a year after the war, Dolan. But here—here's the part I like best. You must have decided to settle down then. The next line I've got on you is in New York. An Army friend of yours—a colonel—had given you a job in his advertising agency. You fell in love with and married a model—and a beautiful one, too— " He checked his notebook. "—Randall, her name was. Dusty Randall. Things went along smoothly for a while. But you couldn't stand the routine of a steady, respectable job, Dolan. The old, old story. You began drinking a little too much. You became suspicious of your wife and jealous of the fact that she was making three times as much money as you.

"One night you got back from an out-of-town trip twelve hours earlier than you were expected. You opened the door of your apartment. The ex-colonel, your boss, your benefactor, was sitting in your favorite chair. He was wearing the dressing-gown your wife had given you the Christmas before. He was drinking your whisky. Your wife Dusty was asleep, or passed out, on the studio couch in the living-room. She was naked. You almost, but not quite, killed your benefactor, the ex-colonel, with your fists. It was a fairly messy do. The papers loved it. Beautiful Model— Outraged Husband, and so forth. The *News* and the *Mirror* ate it up.

"Before you'd even got your divorce you went back into the Army. You were sent to Korea, badly wounded, hospitalized for more than a year—and here we are."

He stood there grinning at me.

I realized that my teeth were clenched. I could feel a vein throbbing in my forehead. It's like taking a blow in the solar plexus to have an almost total stranger tell you things about yourself that you've almost forgotten. The stuff he'd given me wasn't a hundred-percent true. But it was all close enough to hurt.

"How—"

Ringo interrupted me. "I had your wallet, don't forget, Dolan. Your Army discharge, and so on. Names and addresses. Don't you ever throw anything away?" He waved his notebook. "The rest of this information took exactly three long-distance calls. I've got friends here and there, you know. It's my business to know everything about everybody in Carter County, Dolan. Especially big lugs who come through here with chips on their shoulders. And more especially prospective employees." He waved a hand at the filing cabinets across the room. "Everybody in Carter County, Dolan. I know what makes 'em tick. I know the state of their finances, their health—everything. I know who's cheating with whose wife. I know their secret vices." His eyes were glittering again. His voice rose to an almost shrill tone. "And that's why I'm in power, Dolan! Because knowledge plus strength is power! And if you come with me you'll share this power!"

This was a setup here. This was a great spot for a man in my frame of mind. Ringo was offering me first-class accommodations on his own private gravy train. This was ripe. But perhaps a little overripe. The Gestapo, I thought as I glanced at Ringo's filing cabinets. The Gestapo or the MVD and their secret files, their dossiers. I couldn't make up my mind. There was a loud knock at the door.

"Come in," Ringo said.

The door swung open. Loy Bailey thrust his red face and his pot-gut into the room. All the frustration I had experienced that morning by having been kept consistently on the defensive by Rand Ringo exploded

in a blind and unreasoning rage. Here at last was a
chance for action without words. My cheek throbbed
where Bailey had hit me. I could smell the stink of the
tobacco juice he had spit at me. I could feel the sting of
that wet towel as I went for him. And I almost shouted
with exultation at the good feel of my right fist driving
into his pudgy face.

He went down.

I relaxed for a moment then and half-turned away
from him, then saw Ringo move quickly toward him,
a snarl on his face. He kicked the gun from Bailey's
hand—the gun he had pawed from his pocket as I had
turned.

"Goddamn you, Loy," Ringo shouted, "won't you
ever learn that's not the way to do things?"

Maybe I should have thanked Ringo. He'd
probably saved my life. I shrugged and turned to the
window. I saw Gloria Ringo walking down the wide
lawn toward the river. A breeze was rippling her hair.
At the sight of her proud body and her rhythmical
walk, a warmth crept over my body and I made up my
mind. I turned to Ringo.

"I'll take your job," I said. Then I pointed to Loy
Bailey, who was sitting up on the floor now, moaning
softly. "And tell this son of a bitch if he ever lays a
hand on me again I'll kill him!"

Ringo's face was a mocking, smiling mask. He went
to his desk, scribbled something on a pad, tore the
sheet off, and handed it to me. "Take this to Al
Hastings—in town," he said. "He'll take care of you.
I'll call you when I need you."

I took the note, stuffed it into a pocket, and left
Ringo's office. Halfway down the dark hall I sensed,
rather than heard, someone behind me. I turned. Billy
stood in the shadows at the far end of the hall. She
started toward me. I waited for her to reach me.

"Hello, hero." She gave me a big smile.

"What are you doing here?"

"Do you always make like Galahad when you meet strange women?"

I'd had a hard night and an eventful morning and I was in no mood to kick it around. "I asked you a question, Billy."

She stared at me. "I'm his ever-loving wife, that's what. Ringo's. I'm Mrs. Rand Ringo. Pretty name, isn't it? Packs a lot of wallop."

I'd had enough for one day. I got out of there.

Chapter Three

Al Hastings ran a real estate and personal loan company in town—and I supposed that belonged to Ringo, too. Ringo had called in before I got to Hastings's office. Hastings gave me the VIP treatment. He yes-sirred me out of his office and into his car and for three miles out of town and down a clay road through an orange grove. At the end of the clay road was a little bungalow made of weather-beaten cypress. The bungalow was nestled right into the edge of the grove and it was fronted by a narrow lawn that sloped to the shore of a lake.

"Here it is," Hastings said. "Belongs to Mr. Ringo. Man who used to own this grove built it. Sorry kind of a fellow. Mr. Ringo held mortgages on this grove and the man couldn't keep up his payments. House hasn't been used much since then. Sometimes a Yankee'll come in to see Mr. Ringo and he'll stay out here. Fishing's fine—bass, bream, and specs. Boat and motor on a trailer in the garage. Rods and reels and everything you need in the closet off the front room. Mr. Ringo says you're to stay here as long as you want."

It looked—from the outside, at least—like the sort of a place every man who's ever been on the lam, who's put in years in foxholes and barracks and ships and hotels and crummy apartments and cheap boardinghouses must dream about. A great little spot. Papaya trees and avocados and guavas and mangoes taking over where the grove left off. Flame vine groping for the eaves on the sunny side of the house. Rich warm soil and greenness and privacy. Nothing fancy—just solid. And very lovely. I had a peaceful, contented feeling just looking at it. My wheels were spinning. A place like this, I was thinking, with the right sort of a woman to go with it, and the right sort of a job, and ...

I pinched these thoughts in the bud. Dolan, Dolan, I thought. You know all about this thing called domestic bliss. Remember? Remember Dusty sprawled drunk and naked on her back on that couch with her arms over her head? Remember the wanton look of her as she slept? And remember how, after you'd decided not to kill Stephens and had simply left him sobbing through pulpy lips, you lifted her in your arms and carried her to your bedroom and took her then as she had never, to your knowledge, been taken before: roughly, viciously—hurting her, defiling her, hearing her screams turn into moans. Remember how you left her, with her sprawled thighs trembling—looking like the mother of all whores? Remember ...?

And remember the sounding off you'd done in the hospitals about the steady, respectable jobs? There had always been a group of you who'd been through the Big One and had gone back for more in Korea. You were the elite in all the hospitals. For the birds, you'd told them. Listen, you guys, you'd said, I want something big and I want something soft, and whether or not it's strictly legitimate is of no concern to me. How many five-percenters, just for instance, have gotten rich while we've been lying in some stinking hole? How many draft dodgers do you know who've made small fortunes in the past ten years? You've heard about the movie stars with the ruptured ear drums, haven't you? And the young Rotarians with football knees and with fathers who know a Senator?

All right. They've gotten theirs. But there's one thing we've got that they haven't got.

When you've seen Marines floating ass-up and bloated inside a coral reef, and when you've seen a G.I. who died lonesome, with his hands frozen to an M-1, and when you've seen Gooks piled like cordwood in front of a thirty caliber air-cooled machine gun, with what's left of an eighteen-year-old kid from a farm in Kansas slumped over it—then you've got a hardness inside, and a driving desire to look out for yourself, and the know-how to do it, too. These are the things we've got that the others haven't got. And that's just about all we've got. I don't know about you guys, you'd told them, but I figure there are ways of making these things pay off.

Hastings was looking at me curiously. "Like the place?"

"It'll do," I told him.

"You'll find everything you need here. Come on inside."

There wasn't much to it, but there was all I needed—and more. Mostly front room, with a big fireplace, a Capehart combination radio and phonograph, and shelves of books and records. An all-electric kitchen, a big bedroom and bath on the front of the house, a small bedroom and bath on the back. It was perfect. There was even beer in the refrigerator. I opened a can for Hastings and one for myself. We went back into the front room.

"I don't want to forget this," Hastings said. He groped in a pocket for a fat wallet, cracked it, pawed out a slip of paper, and handed it to me. It was a deposit slip from the Cartersville Farmers' Exchange Bank. A single entry on the slip showed that five thousand dollars had been deposited in a checking account in my name.

I played it straight, dead pan.

Hastings sounded disappointed. "That's an advance on your salary, Mr. Ringo said to tell you."

"It'll do," I said, "for a while."

We went back to town then. I gathered my gear from Cartersville's Home Away From Home, tossed my bag in the back seat of my Ford, and headed for my new home. I had no orders to report to anyone or to do anything. As a matter of fact I didn't even know what I was supposed to do when the time came. I decided to just let it ride. I stopped off in a grocery store and stocked up on provisions and supplies. Then I went home, got the boat—a fourteen-foot runabout—into the lake, picked a casting rod and reel from the half-dozen in the closet, gassed the 5-h.p. Johnson kicker, and took off down the lake like a man without a worry in the world.

The shoreline at the far end of the lake was serrated into small coves. Bay and swamp myrtle grew thick to the water's edge, and hoary cypresses, like old men wading, lifted their knobby knees from the water as far as twenty yards from the shoreline. Lily pads— bonnets—choked the coves, and the whole place looked good and fishy. I shut down the kicker, let the boat drift, picked a topwater lure from the tackle box, and started dropping it gently onto the open spots of water behind the cypresses and between the bonnets.

The sun was low and there was no breeze and when my plug hit open water it was like shattering orange and rose and mauve colored glass. An otter, fishing for his supper, slid noiselessly headfirst down a mudbank into the water. A didapper popped his ugly, snakelike head and neck from the water fifty feet from my boat, saw me, and submerged. Two limpkins left their roost in the top branches of a swamp maple and became airborne on wings that paused at the top of their back-swing, as if on gears, to gather strength for their powerful downward thrust.

I fished lazily, absorbing the peace and the beauty of the spot. A bass, and a good one, too, rose to my lure as it settled to the water on my tenth or twelfth cast. I felt that I had hooked him firmly and I let him make his run and when he slacked off I started taking in line. The line came hard and I realized the bass had fouled it in the bonnets. The boat was drifting the wrong way and the bass was thrashing among the pads. There was a canoe paddle in the boat and I sweated with that with one hand, trying to reach the place where my line was fouled. I had almost reached it when I felt the line go slack and I knew the bass had outsmarted me and was gone.

From then on I cast in more open water. In forty-five minutes I had taken three bass averaging, I guessed, four pounds, and had lost another when he'd fouled my line on a cypress stump. I had taken all the fish I could use and I relaxed and drifted, thinking.

Dusty Randall, I thought. Ringo had dredged up that morning the one person in my life whom I could never, I knew—as long as I lived—forget. The memory of my wife roiled and yeasted in me, and roused conflicting emotions that I could neither control nor understand. Bitterness and yearning, and love and hate, and desire and repulsion, and warmth and coldness—a reaching out and a drawing back. I remembered the first time I'd seen her. One of my jobs for the agency was to tag along with the photographers when they took the pictures for our ads. We were working on an automobile account and the layout called for sand dunes and ocean, and the shots were being made at Montauk Point.

I got there a little late: the shooting had started and Dusty and a male model were doing things around the car—getting in, getting out, leaning against fenders, waving to friends, kissing—and then I really noticed Dusty. Her photogenic figure was a little too thin, and her mouth was a little too wide, and her cheekbones were a little too high—but the combination of these features—plus cat-green eyes—was breathtaking. I was attracted to her right from the start.

We made a little polite conversation during the day and that night—we were all staying in a motel there— I hung around after dinner waiting for Dusty to make an appearance. She didn't show. I knocked on the door of her quarters and was asked in.

She was alone. She was wearing gray flannel slacks and a peach-colored sweater. Her dark hair fell loosely across her shoulders. Her green eyes shone. She put down the book she had been reading.

"Well, the young advertising genius. Tell me, Mr. Dolan, are you rich?"

I grinned at her. "Lousy with the stuff. What I draw a week makes the hundred and twenty-five bucks a day we're paying you look like peanuts. And I love to spend it. I can crack a five-dollar bill and have the change spent in three days. I don't care *what* I do with it."

"What a catch. Rich and beautiful. You are beautiful, you know, darling—if you like them king-sized, with shoulders and slightly broken noses and crooked grins. When I look at men like you I think society should be reorganized. We ought to live like bees—with every woman a queen. The males should be divided into workers and drones. You should be a drone, darling, with your sole purpose in life the combined satisfaction of women and the propagation of the race. Come in, but don't stay long. I'm busy."

"Come on. Come with me. We'll look at the ocean."

"Why?"

"I like to look at the ocean."

"How drunk are you?"

"Cold sober."

She slanted her eyes at me. She hesitated for a moment. "You look like a nice guy," she said. "But I've got no time for nice guys." Then she shrugged her

shoulders. "I guess I *could* use a little fresh air," she
said. "I'll go with you—but not for long." She
reddened her lips, wrapped a scarf around her hair,
and lighted a cigarette. "Let's go," she said.

We walked across the road and found a path
through the dunes and walked along the beach. It was
a warm night and the moon lay broadly on the water,
and the rhythm of the sloping waves put my thoughts
in motion. Dusty reached for my hand.

"You're sort of a moony guy, Dolan," she said. "Of
what do you moon, my friend?"

I squeezed her hand. "Nothing. *Nada.*"

"Come on. Give."

"I guess I was thinking about something I once
saw."

"Let's have it."

"Once I was in Honolulu," I said, "and I took a
little boat to Maui, just to look it over. One morning,
at daybreak, I was walking along an empty beach 'way
down the island—I guess this reminded me of it—and
I heard a hell of a trampling, crashing noise in the
woods beyond the beach. I sat behind a log and
watched and waited. A herd of wild horses came
galloping, single file, out of the trees and onto the
beach, led by a big red stallion. They ran on the beach,
playing, and into the sea. The sun was coming up
behind them. Their manes flew and they tumbled and
cavorted and whinnied—they were just like kids—kids
with rippling muscles and a rhythm from out of this
world. And I sat there and watched them, and then
suddenly, as suddenly as they had come, they—"

Her voice was gentle as she interrupted me:
"Dolan—"

I looked at her. Her eyes were soft. She went into
my arms easily, her body warm and curving against
mine, her fingers caressing my face. I kissed her then,
and the wide mouth responded eagerly to my lips, and
the stars in the sky were bright and brittle, and I could

feel the warm, pounding blood of her body. I wanted her. And I knew that she wanted me. But there was something very lovely and very special about the way things were between us at that moment and I didn't want to destroy it. I took her hand and led her through the dunes and back to the motel.

Wild horses and lovely, special moments! Christ how she must have laughed at me!

I shook my head to clear it of memories of Dusty Randall. It was getting dark and I cranked the outboard and headed home. I beached the boat and covered it with a tarp I found in the bow. I went to the house, turned up the lights, found an LP recording of the Toscanini version of Beethoven's Ninth, started it, and turned it up loud enough to hear in the kitchen. I'd found bourbon in a kitchen cabinet. I cracked a jug of it and made a tall highball with plenty of ice and not too much water, and started cleaning my fish. I wrapped four fat fillets in waxed paper and put them in the refrigerator and left the other two out for my dinner.

I finished my drink, made another, turned the Beethoven over and had a hot shower. I dressed in soft moccasins, a pair of old and faded G.I. slacks, and a T-shirt. I was feeling good. This was really living, I thought—especially for a man who had waked up lonely in a country jail that morning. After the Beethoven I looked for some Mozart but couldn't find any, so I settled for Debussy. I sat in an easy chair and listened and I didn't like it as well as the Beethoven, but it was still good. I was thinking about a third highball to nurse while I cooked my fish and made coffee and a salad, when I heard a knock at the door.

I opened the door. It was Billy Ringo.

"You never know," I said.

"Aren't you going to ask me in?"

"Does it make sense?"

"Are *you* afraid of him too?"

That did it. "Come in," I said.

This time she was dressed in some sort of a flaring peasant skirt and her hair was caught up in the back with that ribbon again and lots of smooth, tanned skin showed above the blouse she was wearing. I grinned at her as I pulled the shades.

"After all, the boss's wife—"

Her voice was flat. "You're going to stay here? In this lousy town?"

"I might like it here."

"You're a fool, Dolan!"

"Could be. Drink?"

She nodded. She sat on the sofa and I went to the kitchen, made a drink for her and a fresh one for myself. I wondered why she had come. I wondered what sort of a marriage she and Ringo must have. The night before she had been drunk in a cheap country gambling joint—though the place did, it was true, belong to her husband. Tonight she comes busting in on a man she hardly knows. I remembered Ringo's boast that he knew everything about everybody in Carter County. How much, I wondered, did he know about his own wife?

I took the drinks into the front room, tuned the juke down so that the music was a muted background, watched Billy gulp her drink, and said, "Why did you come here?"

"Maybe I like it here." She shrugged and smiled. "Maybe you interest me, Dolan. Maybe I like your face. You've been hurt and your face is hard, but there's feeling there under the hardness, and it comes out when you grin. You can't hide it."

"Women all like to think they can see past the things that show," I said. "Gives 'em a feeling of superiority."

"You don't think much of women, do you?"

"Love them. In their place."

"Where's that?"

"Bed, mainly."

"You like to seem rugged, don't you, Dolan? I think it's an act."

I didn't want this thing to get out of hand. I changed the subject. "You don't seem to think much of this section of the country. If you don't like it here, why don't *you* leave?"

Her voice was flat. "Because it's too late for me to leave. It's not too late for you to leave, but it will be for you too—if you stick around."

I grinned. "I'm a big boy, mother."

She went on in that flat, detached voice. "You won't believe me. You think I sound as if I were reading lines from a third-rate bleeder. *Nobody* will believe me. You think that if I wanted to leave badly enough I *would* leave. Let me tell you this, pal. I've tried leaving. The first time I left he had me picked up in Miami Beach ten hours later. Ringo, my loving spouse, my Lord and Master, my lover. The next time I got as far as New York. He had men waiting at the plane at La Guardia to bring me back. He beat me that time, Dolan. He whipped me. And he told me that if I ever tried leaving again he'd kill me. And he would, too."

Her drink was gone. This time I brought the jug with me. I poured her a healthy slug. I wanted to hear her story but I wasn't buying too much of it. I'd heard these frustrated wives spill their tall tales before. But any poop I could get on my new employer might be worthwhile. I'd get it, evaluate it, and, if any of it seemed credible, I'd file it away for future reference.

Suddenly, surprisingly, Billy was on her feet. "Look at me, Dolan. Look at me!" She stood tall and straight before me and ran her hands slowly, caressingly, in a preening, downward motion, past her molded breasts, across her softly rounded belly, along her flaring, vital hips. "Look at me. I'm still good, aren't I, Dolan? Aren't I?"

"But very good," I said.

"You should have seen me. You should have seen me before."

She sat down. I knew she was dying to give me her story and I wouldn't stop her. "All right," I said. "Let's have it."

She sipped her drink. "This is the way it was with me. This is the way it was and I hate to even talk about it. The flat I lived in in Chicago was hot in the summer see, and cold in the winter, and it was small and ugly. There were my mother and my father and three of us kids—I was the oldest. When I was sixteen and telling the bartenders I was eighteen, I started running with this guy who sold real estate. I'd met him at a dance. He drove a Cadillac convertible and he was a flashy dresser—you know the type: clothes all tailor-made with plenty of drape, two-toned shoes.... He asked me to marry him, and I said I would.

"My old man hit the ceiling; my mother started moaning. I was too young, they said. They hardly knew the guy. He wasn't Catholic. If I married him they'd never speak to me again. I said fine, that's just fine, you're not ever speaking to me again—you and the whole, shabby, bead-counting lot of you. And so I married my big-time operator—Shultz, his name was, Harry Shultz. I married him, and thirty minutes after the ceremony he threw me down on a hotel bed and raped me.

"For a week I was terrified of him. Then I started hating him. I can't tell you how I hated him and the dirty little things he did. He couldn't talk of anything but the women he'd had, and how much better they were than I was. He had a dozen expensive suits, see, yet most mornings before he went to work he'd smell the armpits of the shirt he'd worn the day before to see if he could get away with it one more day. He wouldn't shave on week-ends, and on Mondays my face would be raw from his slobbering love-making. Dirty little things like that.

"One Saturday afternoon he came home with twelve-hundred dollars in cash. I don't know what he was doing with it. He was that way—liked to flash a roll. He put the money on the dresser. I made him a drink and sat on his lap and talked him into going to bed with me. When he was in the bathroom later I took the twelve hundred dollars and I ran. I ran like hell! I took a taxi to the airfield and got there just in time to get aboard a New York plane.

"I've never seen him since. He finally divorced me."

"Rough deal," I said.

She stared at me. "I didn't know how good I had it. Compared to Rand Ringo, Harry Shultz was a saint."

I wanted to hear more about Ringo. And Gloria. But I didn't want to push her. There was plenty of time.

"You can guess how long I lived in New York with what was left of that twelve hundred," she said.

I nodded.

"I took a job modeling in a wholesale house on Seventh Avenue. I didn't mind the work so much, but the guy I worked with—a man old enough to be my father—started getting ideas. And when I wouldn't play house with him he fired me.

"I'd met a young kid photographer on Eleventh Street. He went in for all this artistic stuff—you know—garbage cans in tenement alleys, old men dozing in doorways, murky looking nudes, things like that. I did a lot of modeling for him. I thought he was crazy, but he was good to me. He made some glamour pictures of me and took me to see John Robert Powers, the model guy. Mr. Powers said I was okay and so I registered with him, and—"

"Excuse me," I said. "You ever know a kid called Dusty Randall?"

"I knew of her. She was, still is, I guess, a top fashion model. Strictly Louise Dahl Wolf, Toni Frissell,

Richard Avedon stuff. My God, the money she makes! Why?"

"I just wondered," I said. "I haven't seen her pictures around lately. Go ahead."

"Well, the Powers office called me a few times for jobs, and they wanted me to make the rounds of all the photographers in town and leave pictures, and I figured, well, I didn't *have* to do that. I was meeting a lot of exciting men and there were dates every night: Stork Club, Morocco, Copacabana—you know."

The old story. It made me feel a little sad. I'd seen it in operation. It's always open season on these beautiful dumb kids, fresh in town. They're wined and they're dined and the glitter gets them and before they know it their heels are round. Some of them get smart in time to make the grade. The rest of them nurse a heartache all their lives. Model to movie queen, model to call girl. It's the chance they take. The lucky ones go home and marry the guy who will inherit his old man's business some day. But the country club will never be the Stork Club. The husband gets a little balder every day and the kids have snotty noses. Things were never like this in New York. I knew the story. But Billy wanted to tell it and I wouldn't stop her. The next step—the inevitable next step—was the guy from C.B.S. Television or the guy who was putting fifty thousand bucks into George S. Kaufman's new show.

But Billy's guy was from a picture company—the New York office. And then came the shack job—and who could blame her? A kid—a not-too-smart kid, but a beautiful, eager kid, with a vital body—in New York for the first time. Stardust in her eyes and the wolves howling at her door. A sudden exposure to big-time glamour, plus flattery and promises that she has no way of knowing are false. The racking memory of a grubby childhood and a marriage to a heel. Who could blame her? It could have happened to Dusty Randall if Dusty had not been possessed of a hard core of sophistication. Dusty was a tramp. She liked men and she collected them. But she was too smart, too cynical, too worldly, ever to have been collected.

And with Billy's shack job came, of course, the charge accounts at Saks' and Hattie Carnegie's and Bergdorf Goodman's, and the studies at Madame somebody-or-other-with-a-Russian-name's dramatic school in the East Fifties, where she was taught to roll vowels from her diaphragm and simulate a llama and an empty tube of toothpaste. And the promise of a screen test that was never fulfilled because the guy wasn't quite big enough to spend fifteen thousand bucks of the company's money just to keep his own private piece happy. And then, finally, the showdown, the breakup, that was recorded for immortality in six words by Walter Winchell.

Then the string of temporary attachments—because it's so hard to work after having been kept. And always, in the offing, there was a screen test, or a chance to read for a show. And this nice older man—the president of some big company—she'd met him at a party—who asked her on a cruise on his private yacht from Ft. Lauderdale to Havana. Strictly on the up and up. Several other young people going along. He just liked the spirit of young people. Liked to have them along. Made *him* feel young again.

And when she was at sea she discovered that the only other young person was a willowy youth with limp wrists and soft eyes and slightly rouged lips, and when she found out that it was planned that all three of them were to sleep in the nice older man's outsized bed in his stateroom that was, by the way, full of pornographic paintings and photographs and statuary, she ran to her own stateroom, locked the door, and didn't come out until they docked the next morning in Miami.

And so she was in Miami—broke. She registered in one of these big loads in Miami Beach. She called her

picture company friend. She got his secretary and she
heard him tell his secretary that he was out. Then, and
always. She called her photographer friend—the one
who made artistic pictures. He must have been drunk,
or something. He said some crazy thing about how you
can't make a silk purse out of a sow's ear, and then he
hung up. She called a couple of other gentlemen friends
and they were all rushing out to keep an appointment,
or late for a business conference, and they all hoped
she had a nice vacation. The weather was lousy in New
York and they all envied her.

And so she put on her best swim suit and went
downstairs to the pool.

"And that's where I met Rand Ringo."

She drank nervously.

"Take it easy," I said.

"He was at the pool. I should never have gone
there. I should never have—"

Her voice was rising, almost hysterically. "God, he
was a handsome man. Five years ago, and the
shoulders on him, and you've seen those eyes, and
when he looked at me I went all warm inside. And he
was so kind, I thought, and so gentle and
understanding. And he brought me back here. He said
he'd been so lonesome since his wife had died. He
showed me his home—the swimming pool, the stables,
the boats. And he never touched me, never—all that
time. And I guess I fell in love with him. Fell in love,
really, for the first time. And when he asked me to
marry him I said I would, and—"

She started sobbing.

"For God's sake, Billy," I said. I went to her. I
couldn't help it. "Billy, for God's sake—" I sat beside
her. She turned to me. I wanted to stroke those tears
away and I knew that I could surely do it. I wanted her
in my arms but I knew she was poison. I'd reminded
myself, when she'd first stepped into that room, that
this was not for me. She was Ringo's wife and I

wouldn't touch her. Hands off, no trespassing, *verboten*. Her arms were around my neck now. I forced them away. I stood and crossed the room to the bottle. I slopped bourbon into my glass and started it to my lips. Billy was beside me, tugging at me, turning me towards her, glomming onto me. Her breasts were hard and demanding against my chest and her thighs strained against mine as we stood together. My glass shattered on the floor as I took her in my arms, and I tasted the wet saltiness of her lips as she forced them against mine. Her sobs turned into moans and her tongue was quick as I lifted her into my arms and took her into my bedroom. And when, later, I turned on the light and looked at her the fear had gone from her eyes and she looked at me sleepily and said, "You're my kind of a guy, Dolan."

And then we both heard it together, the crackling noise of a small branch breaking—just outside the bedroom window. There was an inch-and-a-half between the bottom of the shade and the window sill. Billy stifled a scream. I groped for my slacks, then on the dresser for my .45 and a flashlight. I ran for the porch.

But I was too late. The row of azaleas that grew under the bedroom window had been pretty well trampled. Heavy footsteps, men's footsteps, were in the azalea bed. But whoever it was had gone. I had a quick look around the house, then went back inside.

After Billy left I made myself a quick sandwich and poured a glass of milk. Then I showered again, stuck my .45 under my pillow, and went to bed.

I was dog-tired. But I didn't sleep very well.

Chapter Four

I was pretty jumpy the next day. I imagined that word had gotten back to Ringo that his wife had been with me. I was geared for trouble and I wondered why it didn't come. Ringo called me three days later, on a Friday. He wanted to see me. His voice was friendly, casual. Perhaps he didn't know about Billy. Or maybe he knew and just didn't care. Whatever it was, Ringo had me guessing, off-balance. And I didn't like being off-balance.

Loy Bailey was in Ringo's office when I got there. Ringo greeted me in a friendly way. I looked closely at him. His face was a smiling mask. His thoughts were hidden. Bailey grunted at me. On a sudden impulse I said, "Where were you around eleven o'clock last Tuesday night, Loy?" I grinned at him.

"The way I figure it, it's none of your goddamn business." His ugly face didn't show a thing. "Why?"

Ringo was looking at me, question marks in his eyes.

"Skip it," I said. "Just curious—that's all."

"Sit down, Dolan." Ringo said. He shoved a package of Camels at me. I took one, lighted it, and sat down.

"In the quarters east of town there's a nigra named Sam Foster," he said.

I waited, watching him.

"Sam runs our bolita game out there."

"Goddamn Yankee nigger," Bailey grunted.

"I'm doing the talking," Ringo said.

I grinned at Bailey. He glared back at me, murder in his eyes.

"Do you understand bolita?"

"Numbers, isn't it? I've heard of it in Georgia and South Carolina. I'm a little hazy—"

"It's our most profitable"—Ringo smiled—"shall we say, sideline? It's sometimes known as nighthouse. We have five houses in the county. Sam Foster runs one of them. There's a separate throwing every night at each of the five houses. You can buy your ticket for the throwing at any or all of the houses. You bet a number from one through a hundred. A dollar on a winning number will get you seventy."

"Nice odds," I said. "For the house."

"We're not in this business for our health," Ringo said. "And it's plenty big. Like all numbers rackets, bolita thrives on the underprivileged and the ignorant. Unfortunately"—Ringo winked at Bailey—"Carter County has more than its share of the underprivileged and the ignorant—due to its big nigra population mainly, plus the number of transient fruit workers and field hands.

"Now the Dade County boys and the Orange County boys have had their eyes on us for a long time. They're big, well-organized groups—both members of nationwide syndicates. The Dade County mob takes its orders from the present bosses of the old Capone regime. So far, I've been able to keep them out. It hasn't been easy and it hasn't been cheap. I've had to buy some pretty important politicians in this state. But there's going to be trouble, Dolan. And that's one reason why you're working for me."

"I've been in trouble before. Plenty."

"I just wanted to brief you. It might get rough."

I grinned at him.

"All right. About the bolita. I said that there was a throwing every night at each of the five houses. Here are the mechanics of the throwing: it's done in the presence of as many players as want to be on hand. A hundred wooden balls, each one no bigger than a big marble, numbered one to a hundred, are dumped— while the players watch—into a cloth bag. The bag is sealed. The house man tosses the bag to one of the players. The player fingers the balls—through the cloth—until he's got one that feels good. The house man ties it off from the others, cuts it away—and there's your winning number."

"Any rigging?" I asked.

"It's possible," Ringo said. "A good house man can palm a number that has gotten a big play. There are two or three other methods—" Ringo cleared his throat. I had a feeling that this sort of talk was offending his delicate sensibilities. He apparently saw nothing evil in lifting a mathematical thirty per cent from the gambling populace of Carter County, but he was sensitive about cheating. I couldn't see much difference, myself. A ream job was a ream job— whether partial or complete.

"About Sam Foster," Ringo said.

"I'm listening," I said.

"Sam has always done a good job for us out there. He's made us a lot of money. A nigra will buy a bolita ticket with the last dime in his house—if he's allowed to. But Sam has gotten a lot of funny ideas lately. He's been reading the wrong kind of literature; he's been talking to the wrong kind of people. He's gotten some sort of a biggety idea that the nigras around here are being taken advantage of. He won't rig his game. He won't take bets from those he thinks can't afford to bet. His receipts have fallen off out there—"

"Let me handle the black bastard!" Bailey said.

Ringo's voice was soft, rich, Southern, friendly. "I said I was doing the talking, Loy."

The sheriff grunted.

"I just don't know what's happened to Sam," Ringo continued. There seemed to be a sincere note of regret in his voice. "There's the loan business that Al Hastings has been running, for instance. You know Al—"

I nodded.

"Al's been doing a big business with the nigras of this section. Sam's been talking against Al. He's been saying that Al's a loan shark, that he would like nothing better than to get them on a financial hook and keep them working for him the rest of their natural lives. He's been telling those people to come to him if they have to have money. He's been loaning out money half again as cheap as Al can loan it—and in many cases loaning it free. Al's getting mighty upset. I happen to be interested in Al's business and I'm getting mighty upset, too."

"Why don't you just can him? Get yourself a new bolita boy?" I asked.

"I'm surprised at you, Dolan. The nigras all love Sam Foster out there. If I let Sam Foster go and put another man in his place I believe the nigras would refuse to play bolita. I'm really surprised at you. I'd thought your thinking might be a little more subtle than Loy's here. If I'd let him, Loy would drum up some sort of a minor offense and take Sam to jail, and then he and his deputies would go over him with their leather straps and their hoses and their fists until even his mother wouldn't recognize him. Then Loy would send him home. And then every nigra man, woman, and child in the quarters would set him up in their minds as being about one niche lower than Jesus Christ. Don't you see, Dolan?"

His voice took on a throbbing, sincere, almost pleading quality. "These people, the nigras, are not like us. They're children. They must be treated like children— but children with adult vices. Let them work and laugh and play, drink a little, gamble a little, and make plenty of love, and they're happy. That's our responsibility toward the nigras—to let them do these things, to treat them like children: reward them when they're good, punish them when they're bad. But to always keep an upper hand. We've got to guide them, mold them, teach them their proper place in the scheme of things. You show me a nigra who doesn't know his place and I'll show you a nigra who's unhappy."

Ringo stood up and started to pace the floor. His hands were clenched into fists. "You've got to understand that I love these people. And because I love them I understand them. I know that sometimes pretty stringent methods of discipline are necessary to maintain this relationship between the nigras and those of us responsible for their happiness. Sometimes we're forced to do things we hate to do, but must do, to keep the rest of the children in their places and happy. And I'm not talking about your kind of discipline, Loy—or even yours, Dolan. There are more subtle, more refined ways of doing things. And smarter ways, too—ways that won't make a martyr of a man. I've got something special in mind for Sam Foster, if he doesn't stop breeding unhappiness out there."

What a speech! Ringo stopped pacing. He leaned on his desk and stared at me. His eyes were glittering black. "You go out and tell him that, Dolan. You go out and handle this thing in a civilized manner—as Loy here could never do. You go out and throw the fear of God into him, Dolan, in a nice, refined way. You go out and persuade him to quit stirring those people up out there. Explain to him that we want to see our children happy. And drop a hint to him that there's a little special treatment in store for him if he doesn't see things our way. A hint should be enough."

I stood up, thankful for a chance to get out of there. I glanced at Loy Bailey's face. The pig eyes that glared at me were brutal with suppressed rage.

"Let me know how you make out," Ringo said.

I went outside. I started to get into my Ford when I saw Gloria. She was standing among the groping, twisting, downward-thrusting arms of a great banyan. She was looking at me. There was a half-smile of greeting—or was it expectancy?—on her face. I had a sudden desire to shout out at her, to warn her away from those groping, twisting arms before they enfolded her and choked her life away. I shook my head to clear it of such morbid, stupid thoughts. Then I got into my car and drove away.

Sam Foster's house in the quarters was small but neat—freshly painted, with a square of green lawn edged by well-trimmed hedges that stood out like a sore thumb among the litter-strewn dirt yards of his neighbors. I knocked at his door. A big sad-eyed man, quite dark and no longer young, opened the door.

"Sam Foster?"

"Yes, sir."

"I'm Dolan. I work for Mr. Ringo."

His eyes went shadowy.

"Yes, sir?"

"Where can we talk?"

The living-room was almost bare—but neat. Foster led me to a small room off the living-room. A beat-up roll-top desk, two chairs, and a lamp were the furnishings. A .30-30 rifle leaned in a corner.

We sat down. "I think maybe I know why you're here," he said.

"Yes?"

"Why didn't Mr. Ringo come himself?"

"I don't know."

"Coffee?"

"Yes."

"You'll have to excuse me. I live alone." He got up and left the room. I heard him rattling cups and saucers around in the kitchen. Then he called me. "Mr. Dolan—"

"Yes."

"You mind stepping here a minute, sir?"

Sam Foster was standing at his high kitchen window, cups and saucers in his hand. "You mind looking out here a minute. Mr. Dolan?"

I stood beside him and looked out. The shacks in the quarters were all tumbled together, with rutted and pitted clay and dirt roads wandering between and around them. From Sam's window I could see the back yards of eight or ten shacks. These back yards were choked with rusting parts of automobiles and ruined tires and broken bathtubs and privies patched against the weather with old license plates and scraps of tin. On a corner beyond the back yards was a shabby, unpainted beer parlor. Noisy jive blared from its open door and a woman and two men, rolling drunk, were trying to dance, the three of them together, in the road before it. A handful of bare-bottomed pickaninnies played in the road dust with empty beer cans, heedless of the drunken dancers near them.

Sam Foster had been staring at me. "Like it?" he asked.

I turned away without answering him. I went back to his office. Sam followed me with a tray with a battered coffee pot, two cups and saucers, sugar and cream on it. "How do you take it, Mr. Dolan?"

"Sugar and cream."

I didn't quite know how to start. I'd been sent here to throw the fear of God—in what Ringo called a "refined" way—into a cheap bolita operator who was getting too big for his britches. I had expected some sharpie—a nervous, over ambitious, brash, self-seeking rabble-rouser. The quietness, the dignity, the self-possession of this big man with the sad and knowing eyes was throwing me for a loss. I forced myself to remember that this man was a gambler—in the business of running a rotten racket that thrived on the foolish dreams of an ignorant people.

Before I could stop myself I said, "What are you doing in this rotten racket, Sam?" And I could feel the blood rising to my face as I realized the naiveté of my question, like the almost invariable question of a teenage boy who's been with his first whore.

Foster grinned, showing white, even teeth. "I could ask you the same question maybe, Mr. Dolan. But I don't reckon I will."

This thing was getting out of hand. Come off it, Dolan, I thought. You're supposed to be riding herd on this man—and it's he who's doing the riding. You're a guy who's looking out for himself—remember? And you can't do that with a bleeding heart.

"All right, Sam," I said, "I'll lay it on the table. Mr. Ringo says you're talking when you ought to be listening. He says you're stirring up the people out here. He wants you to cut it out. He wants these people out here to operate just as they've always operated. Is that clear?"

"That's clear all right, Mr. Dolan."

"You know what he's talking about? The gambling, the loans, and so forth?"

He nodded.

"And so you'll cut it out?"

"No, sir," he said.

"He asked me to tell you that he had a little special treatment in mind for you if you didn't see things his way."

His eyes were veiled with trouble. "Mr. Dolan, I'm a peace-loving man. I don't want no trouble. But a man has to do what he thinks is right. If he don't, he's lost. My folks out here need help. They need it bad. And I reckon I'll have to keep right on trying to help them. There ain't anybody else."

"Aren't you being a little bit hypocritical?"

"You mean the bolita game?"

I nodded.

"They're going to play bolita, Mr. Dolan. At least until they're educated out of it. And they're going to keep on buying and reading Aunt Min's Dream Book to try and find the lucky number. But with me running the game out here they're going to get a square deal— as square as the game allows. I run it clean. Another man might not. And besides that it makes me enough money to help out where help is needed."

I stood. "You won't take my warning?"

He shook his big head mournfully.

"Foster, you're a goddamned fool."

"Mr. Dolan—you mind if I say something?"

I waited.

He looked me straight in the eyes.

"Mr. Dolan, your heart and your tongue don't meet."

I went home thinking about that one.

Chapter Five

I called Ringo the next day and told him I'd seen and warned Sam Foster. When he asked me about Sam's reaction I hedged. I don't know why I hedged—but I did. I told him I was pretty sure Sam would straighten out and fly right. I asked him if he had any more orders and he laughed at me. "We never hurry down here. I know where to find you when I need you. Take it easy. Relax."

Relax. It wasn't easy to do. I played records and drank beer and fished and swam. I went to town. I spent time in the barber shops and with the loafers in the beer parlors and around the packinghouse loading platforms. I wasn't wasting my time. I was asking questions, discreet questions, and I was putting all the answers together and adding them to what I had seen and what Ringo had told me. And I was getting a pretty good picture of the way Ringo ran the county and what it meant to him financially. What I couldn't understand, however, was the psychological stranglehold that Ringo had over most of the good citizens of Carter County. Everybody knew him. Everybody knew he ran the county. Few seemed to like him. And yet they all seemed to accept his domination of the county as the status quo and they refused to do anything about it. They'd had their noses rubbed in it for so long that they seemed to accept the nose-rubbing as S.O.P.

In the barber shop on the main stem, for instance: I stopped by for the works one morning. It was a shimmering hot morning and sweat glistened from the jowls of the colored shine boy as he slapped his brushes with a boogie beat against a pair of stockman's boots. Flies crawled sleepily on the plate glass window and through this window, across the street, I watched heat waves dancing from the empty concrete of the shuffleboard courts. Old men sprawled on their backsides on benches in the shade of the rubber tree and fanned their leathery faces with straw hats. A flop-eared hound dog sprawled full-length and panting in the seared grass. A barefooted, shirtless boy of four or five was trying to shinny up the public drinking fountain for a drink of cool water. A sign on a post beside the fountain said, *For Whites Only!* and I supposed the city fathers worked on the assumption that "niggers", being "niggers", had no business being thirsty. Not, at any rate, while they were downtown.

While I waited my turn I listened to a red-hot argument going on between two or three of the shirt-sleeved barbers and several of the customers over the gas consumption of several standard makes of automobiles. I figured the argument would expand to include the qualities, good and bad, of these various cars as whole units. It did. Then I waited for it to narrow down to Fords versus Chevrolets. It wasn't long before it did this, too. They couldn't fool me: I'd had these country towns before. Today the Ford supporters were in the majority. They seemed on the verge of winning out when one of the customers—who'd been muffled by a hot towel during the preliminaries—had the audacity to put in a word for a foreign car. With that the Ford and Chevrolet forces buried the hatchet and ganged together in righteous indignation to talk the rebel down.

Next on the agenda was a dirty Truman joke by a fat barber with a South Georgia accent and the first pair of sleeve garters I'd seen in a long time. The joke was an old one that Truman had inherited from Roosevelt and that Roosevelt had, for all I knew, inherited from Hoover. In another year they'd probably be telling it on Eisenhower. The other barbers slapped their thighs and guffawed. The customers either laughed or smiled—depending upon whether they were having a haircut or a shave. I would have laid even money that there wasn't a man in the house who had ever voted, or would ever vote, anything other than a straight Democratic ticket.

And then somebody mentioned Ringo. All private discussions ceased.

"They tell me Ringo gave eight thousand dollars to the Baptists for that new annex they been talking about over there."

Somebody else, said, "Bought the Methodists a new organ last year, didn't he?"

The man who had supported the foreign car said, "You know why, don't you?"

"I reckon because Ringo's a generous man," the fat barber said.

"You weren't born yesterday, were you, Lon?"

The fat barber glared at him. "What are you trying to say?"

The foreign-car man was a heretic, indeed. Or nursing a grudge because of the way the Ford and Chevrolet people had ganged up on him. "I'll tell you why Ringo gives money to the churches of this town. It's the truth, and there are people in this town and county who ought to be told the truth. So I don't give a good goddamn whose toes I'm treading on when I say it. There's a wet-dry vote coming up again in September. Ringo wants this county dry so's he can keep reaming the drinking citizens with his bootleg booze business, that's why. And the bootleg booze business ain't all. Not by a long sight. You got to go to a joint like Joe's Place or the Blue Heron or Adele's if you want a drink. And the first thing you know you've belted a few and you're throwing money into one of Ringo's crap, blackjack, or poker games, or you're ending up in the sack with one of his whores. As long as this county stays dry he's got you coming and going. And who else wants it dry? The churches. And what's more, they *keep* it dry. So why shouldn't Ringo kick in with a few bucks to help the churches? Hellfire, they're keeping him in business!"

This speech seemed to make everybody in the shop uncomfortable. I saw two or three of the men glance nervously at me. None of the men there knew—as far as I could make out—that I worked for Ringo. But, being a stranger, I was suspect.

Lon, the fat barber, wouldn't give ground. "You're beating your gums, Pete," he said, "and you don't know ass from appetite about what you're saying. Ringo's a rich man. Like all rich men he's got plenty of enemies. They say a lot of things about Ringo that just plain ain't so. And even if they was so it wouldn't bother me none. I never seen a man yet forced into a crap game or a barroom or a whorehouse. Live and let live—that's my motto."

They were ganging up on Pete again.

"Ringo's done aplenty for this town!"

"You ain't just a'bird-turding, mister!"

"You don't like it here, Pete, well, why don't you move on down to Miami Beach or some such as that? They say a man can get along good on a hundred dollars a day down there. Barrooms all over the place. And all of 'em full of women in short pants. Hot almighty damn!"

Just then Al Hastings came into the shop. He spotted me. "Morning, Mr. Dolan," he said. "Mr. Ringo called and asked me to tell you to check with him if I saw you. Something's come up he wants you to handle—"

They all heard him.

Pete's face had been shaved. He climbed down from the chair and he glanced at me and there was a sickly little smile on his face. Everybody watched him as he went to the coat rack for his hat. He tried to bluff it out. He tossed a quarter to the colored boy and said heartily, "Well, 'Shine, you getting any strange stuff out there in the quarters nowadays?"

Nobody laughed, and Pete hurried from the shop. Lon said scornfully, "—any son of a bitch'd drive a foreign car—"

"How many gallons of gas you reckon my Plymouth burned between here and Atlanta, Georgia?" somebody said, and they were off again.

I went to call Ringo. It was nothing important. I went home and went back to my record playing, my reading, my fishing, and my swimming. Relax, the man had said. Those were my orders and I tried to comply. But after a few days of this I was restless, lonesome. Billy Ringo hadn't shown again and this suited me fine. I had enough on my mind without worrying about her. I had plenty on my mind. And first and foremost was the fresh memory of Gloria Ringo, and of the passion sleeping behind those slanting black-brown eyes. I went to bed thinking of Gloria and I woke up thinking of her and I knew that I must see her again, hear her speak, touch her, make her come alive.

And so I went to Ringo's on the slight chance that I might see her alone. I ran in luck.

Ben met me at the door. "Mr. Ringo's gone to Miami on business," he told me. "Don't know when he'll be back. Mr. Ringo, he comes and he goes. Miz Ringo, she taken off after lunch, didn't say when she'd be back."

"And Miss Gloria?" I tried to throw the line away.

The old man's liquid brown eyes looked deep into me and I had the feeling then—the same feeling I'd had with Sam Foster, the same feeling I usually have with Negroes—that these people have a depth of perception, a sensitivity to basic emotions and motives, that the rest of us don't have. With Ben this feeling of mine was even more clearly defined. I had an uncomfortable feeling that he was seeing inside me, seeing things that even I, perhaps, was not aware of. And he seemed to approve of whatever it was he thought he saw.

"Miss Gloria, she went on up to the stables. Had her riding britches on. Reckon she taken one of her horses out."

"Oh." I hoped I didn't sound too disappointed.

"Anything I can do for you, Mr. Dolan? Drink? Food?"

"No, thanks, Ben."

"Fresh cool water in the swimming pool."

I wondered why he was being so solicitous.

"I'll come out again, Ben." I turned to leave.

"Yes, sir." He waited until I was out on the lawn. "Got some pretty good hosses up there in the stables."

I turned and looked at him. He was looking the other way.

"Mr. Ringo don't get much of a chance to ride anymore. It's near about all Miss Gloria and Early the stable boy can do to keep them hosses exercised."

"All right, Ben." I grinned at him.

"Miss Gloria, she likes to ride thataway." He waved a skinny arm, then ducked back into the house.

I wasn't dressed for it and I hadn't been aboard a horse for ten years—but these were minor matters. The stable boy was asleep on a bale of hay. I shook him awake. I told him that I was a friend of Mr. Ringo's and that Ben had suggested I take one of the horses out. Early showed me the whites of his eyes, brushed flies away from his sweat-glistening face, and asked me if I had any special horse in mind.

"A gentle one," I said.

"Yessir."

When he had bridled and saddled an elderly looking gelding I swung aboard in what I hoped was a competent manner. "Miss Gloria say which way she was going?"

"Nossir."

Ben had waved toward the river and south. A well-traveled trail outside the corral led in that general direction. I took it. When I was out of Early's sight I nudged my horse into a trot and realized almost immediately that I had forgotten—if I had ever known—how to post. The jouncing was giving my left leg hell. I urged the old boy into an easy canter and this was better.

The trail swung south at the river's edge. I crossed a prairie that opened out and spread westward as far as I could see. There must have been upward of seven hundred cattle in scattered groups on that stretch of prairie, and I wondered, as I saw all the wealth there, at man's greed. Ringo must have, I thought, all the worldly goods that an ordinary man could desire—and yet he must squeeze, bleed, gouge, punish, intimidate practically the entire population of a county for more.

I shrugged these thoughts away. It was of no concern to me. Let me get my share—that was all that mattered to me. This was a rich setup, this Carter County deal. And I, by a great stroke of good fortune, was riding the gravy train. Last week's doubts had dissipated. I was in on a very good thing. I would ride it for what it was worth. I set fifty thousand dollars as my goal. Fifty grand—and I'd kiss Carter County good-by. I'd go farther south. Maybe to Miami, as I'd originally planned. With fifty thousand bucks I could lay low, play it cozy, wait for a real good thing.

Or maybe skip Miami. Go on down the Keys somewhere and buy myself a fishing camp, or an inn, or a motel. Maybe run a game or so in the back room for the good customers, but run it straight, on the up and up. Take it easy and live in the sun.

Or maybe buy a good boat and do a lot of fishing and cruising around. Dry Tortugas, Key West, Bimini, Havana. A man with a good fast boat and the right contacts could do all right for himself in Havana, I'd been told.

Fifty grand. That shouldn't take too long. Ringo was coining it hand over fist. I'd been able to put together a few rough figures from the things Ringo had told me and the things I'd been able to pick up on my own. Ringo's weekly bolita gross must be at least twenty grand, I figured. Small operation, yes, when compared to similar operations in metropolitan areas, but this rural setup was neat, tidy, comparatively cheap to run—and all Ringo's.

And that was just the bolita. There was the other gambling—the crap tables, the blackjack, the poker. The bootleg booze business was smaller, but good. Most of the goods consumed were bought over the county line by citizens of the county—but there were always those who needed a quick jug at eight bucks a fifth.

And then there were the bars, too, in joints like Joe's Place. And the whores: they were Ringo's, too. Whorehouses, as such, were—with one notable exception—non-existent. The girls operated around the country jukes. B-girls. They were there, ostensibly, to drink and dance with the customers. There were always tourist cabins close by. Ten bucks for a quick party or twenty-five for an all-night stand. Ringo's cut was fifty per cent, right down the line.

A setup. Made to order for a man in my frame of mind.

My horse was wheezing. I slowed him to a walk as the trail furrowed into hammock-land—rich, dark soil matted with decaying vegetation. Live oaks and cabbage palms, with an occasional Royal palm lifting its head above the rest. Coolness and dimness below. Fresh marks of hoofs were in the soft soil of the winding trail and I knew that Gloria was somewhere ahead of me. When my horse stopped wheezing I nudged him into his easy canter again.

The trail forked. The hoof marks went left and I followed them. The ground rose gently, and suddenly I was in a clearing on a bluff overlooking the winding river. The weather-whitened bones of a house lay sprawled around the half-crumbled field stone fireplace and chimney in the middle of the clearing. Wild orange trees surrounded the remains of the house. Honeysuckle choked what was left of a well. It was a sad and lonely place. I wondered what sort of a man had settled in this place—and how he had come to grief. I dismounted, looped the reins to a branch of a wild orange tree, and walked around the clearing. Beyond the clearing the trail disappeared into forest again. My leg was stiff from the riding I'd done and I decided to walk for a while.

Just off a sharp turn of the trail I saw a horse, unbridled, unsaddled—but with saddle marks on him—picking at grass under a giant live oak. I walked softy. The horse saw me, but was unconcerned. The ground was spongy as I left the trail. A skink lizard crossed my feet and disappeared into leaves beside me. I could smell water, fresh and sweet, and then I could hear it running. I was in ferns, now—head high, fragrant, damp.

I moved slowly, cautiously. Suddenly, through an opening in the ferns, I saw the moss-grown remains of a cypress spring house. Water, fresh and clean, ran sparkling from its ruined entrance. I took another step forward and caught my breath; I froze to the spot.

The water from the spring ran downhill over a limestone bed and formed a pool. About fifty feet across and thirty feet long. The water in the middle was dark and green and it looked deep. Blood-red hibiscus clamored for attention on the far side of the pool. But they were out-classed. On my side of the pool, ankle-deep in water, in profile to me, stood Gloria Ringo. She was naked. Her hair clung wet and shining to the proud column of her neck, and water glistened from her lovely, thrusting breasts and from her flat belly and her rounded thighs and down the lengths of her long, slim legs—and I wished then that I had never come looking for her. I felt, for the second time in my life, that I was seeing a thing that I was unworthy of seeing. I felt old, and dirty, and ruined, and I knew that I must go, but I couldn't tear my eyes away. I watched her as she poised to dive. She split the water cleanly and swam in long, easy strokes toward the other side of the pool.

When she was halfway across I turned to leave. I cursed my clumsiness as I stepped squarely on a dead limb; it made a cracking noise as it broke. I looked back, into Gloria's frightened eyes, and I said—fumbling for words like a schoolboy on his first date—"I didn't know. I'm sorry—"

She was treading water in the middle of the pool. I was amazed then to see and hear her laugh. "Why are men so clumsy?" she said. "And how did you get here?"

I relaxed and grinned at her. "All men are clumsy when they're caught peeking through keyholes. I followed you here—it was Ben's idea. I had no idea I would find you in—"

She smiled. "In the altogether? Now you know my secret. This is my favorite spot—I come here as often as I can. Ben's an old devil—he loves to stir up trouble. Do you know what my father would do if he knew you had followed me here?"

"I can guess."

"Daddy is of the old school. He'd probably shoot you."

I had no doubt that he would.

"Don't just stand there gawking. Go away. Go back to the clearing. When I'm dressed I'll see you there. We'll ride back together."

"All right." I turned to leave.

"Dolan—"

I turned.

"Exactly how long have you been standing there?"

I grinned. "Long enough."

I saw her cheeks redden and then I turned and left her.

I took off my shirt and let the sun beat hot on my back as I waited for her by the ruins of the old house. And as I waited I marveled at the difference in Gloria's personality when she was away from that ungodly hulk of a house, away from her father. The other times I had seen her she had seemed half-awake; her loveliness had been two-dimensional—a portrait of beauty rather than living beauty. And now, away from that house, away from Ringo, she was vitally alive, her femininity warm, breathing, throbbing; she was a woman who could be touched—and held.

She wore jodhpurs and a white blouse, and the translucent skin of her arms and neck and face glowed with health and well-being and cleanliness. She dismounted and let her horse go free to forage the grass in the clearing. She sat beside me on a fallen beam and together we looked across the top of the forest to the black, winding river.

"Like it here?" she asked me.

"There's a sadness here," I said. "And a loneliness. I wondered what sort of a man cleared this land and built this house."

"He was a wonderful man," she said. "He was a poet who couldn't rhyme. He loved to watch the river from here. He was watching the river when he died. They found him with his back propped against that wild orange tree there. He was facing the river and he was smiling."

"You knew him?"

"A little. I was very young when he died. He was my grandfather."

I said nothing.

"Daddy was born here. He and Grandfather never got along. Grandfather was one of those people who never cared about money. He made a bare living from this place. He hunted and he fished and he read and he raised good hounds and he loved to listen to the sound of their voices as they bayed the moon. And he watched the river. Daddy said he was an old fool. Grandfather told Daddy that money was a false god— and that those who worshiped it would come to an evil end. He'd never come to live with us; he would never accept help from Daddy. He died proudly, watching his river. He'd starved to death. I think he wanted to."

I said quietly, "And how do you feel about your father?" It was a thing I had to know.

Her eyes were defiant. "I love him—of course!"

"Of course."

"He's a good, kind man. He'll do anything for me. He'll give me anything I want."

I remembered Billy Ringo's defiance at the bar at Joe's Place when I had ribbed her about losing so much money at the crap table. "There's plenty where mine came from! All I want!" Gloria's tone of voice now was much as Billy's had been then.

"Are you trying to convince *me*, Gloria?" I asked her. "Or yourself?"

Her eyes flashed. "You can't talk like that about my father! You—"

I interrupted her. "Gloria—I haven't been talking about your father. You've been doing the talking. I've seen his eyes when he's with you. I've seen him touch you." It was a shot in the dark. I watched her closely. "I know he loves you."

Her eyes wouldn't meet mine. "What are you trying to imply?"

"Nothing." I reached for her hand. "Tell me, what do you know about your father's business?"

Her hand went rigid in mine. "I've heard ugly rumors since I got back—if that's what you mean.

They're lies—all of them! I know they're lies! He's in a lot of things besides cattle: citrus, real estate—all kind of investments. And politics, too. That's one reason he's away so much. You ought to know what he does. You work for him. What do you do?"

I hated to lie to her. But I had it to do. I tried to grin and the grin came out crooked. "Well, he's grooming me for sort of a right hand man, you might say. Sort of a contact man. I'm to handle the messy details that your father hasn't time for."

"There. You see?" Her hand went soft in mine.

The subject was red hot, and I changed it. "You just said, 'since I got back.' Where've you been?"

"Oh, I've been leading an exciting, adventurous, lurid existence. Mother died when I was seven—that's thirteen years ago—and Daddy sent me to a convent near Washington. From there I went to a Miss Simpson's Finishing School in Virginia. We raised hell all the time. Movies once a week, heavily chaperoned dances once a month. I finished school last spring. Daddy says I can go to Europe this fall if I want to. He'll send a maiden aunt along to be my duenna. We'll have a gay old time poking around museums and art galleries and going to bed at nine-thirty every night."

"Why doesn't he send Billy with you?"

Her eyes went troubled. "Poor Billy—Daddy tries so hard to be patient. Sometimes I think she's trying to drink herself to death...."

"And so you're going to Europe?"

"Not if I can help it. I want to live a little, Dolan. All this might not suit some women—but I love it here. And when I can't sleep nights, when things start gnawing at me inside, when I wonder what God made me a woman for—then I can ride. Or I can drive the speedboat wide open down the river until I'm calm again inside."

I had trouble with my voice. "Gloria," I said, "I want to tell you something—and I want you to believe me. When I first saw you today—I couldn't breathe. I felt, for the second time in my life, that I was seeing something that I was unworthy of seeing. I felt old, and dirty, and ruined. And—"

She put a hand to my mouth. Her eyes were soft and shining and her full lips were slightly parted. I swept her hand from my mouth and I slid from the beam to the heavy, sweet-smelling grass beside it, and I pulled her with me. As I pressed my lips to hers something, somewhere inside me, was saying, *Goddamn you, Dolan, don't do it, don't do it*, and I knew that wild horses couldn't keep me away from her. The blouse was off, and then the bra, and the nipples were rosy and firm and she moaned softly and trembled as I kissed them, and she said, "Don't, Brad— don't darling," as I loosened the belt of her jodhpurs. And in a moment there was the sweet, caressing feel of silk against thighs and then the world spun crazily, and I was man—Almighty Man—as tall as a Georgia pine and as strong as a team of horses. I felt Gloria's nails rip the flesh of my shoulders but it didn't hurt and then the world spun to a stop on the last note of Gloria's cry and we lay trembling in each other's arms.

After a while we sat up. Gloria stared at me with wonder in her eyes. "Damn you for doing that, Dolan," she whispered.

"Why?"

She wouldn't answer me. "Come on," she said. She took my hand and together we returned to the spring pool in the forest and we stripped again, and plunged together into the cool, refreshing water. We swam and dived and played, laughing like kids, and when my breath came short I pulled myself from the pool to a shady, grassy ledge beside it and Gloria joined me.

She took my hand. "You're a funny guy, Dolan," she said. "I'd like to know what makes you tick. I get a feeling that you're looking for something that you've never found. True?"

"Isn't it true of everybody?"

"Some people never look."

"I guess maybe I'm looking for answers."

"To what?"

"Anything. Everything."

She was silent for a moment, thinking. "A little while ago you were talking about seeing me here on the edge of this pool. You said that was the second time in your life you'd seen something you felt unworthy of seeing. When was the first time?"

I grinned at her. "You'll think I'm nuts."

"Anything but that."

"That first time was one of the few times I've felt close to finding an answer."

"Yes?"

"I was a kid then, see—not even twenty. I was traveling across the country, east to west, job to job, on the lam, moving because I couldn't stay put. Looking for answers. Looking, listening. I met a lot of strange people with a lot of strange answers. I listened to revolutionists in the parks of the big cities. I met ex-Wobblies and ex-ham-and-eggers and crackpots and cranks in hobo jungles and on skid rows the breadth of the country. I knew Mennonites in the Carolinas and Mormons in Utah and Baptists in Nebraska and sun-worshipers in New Mexico and ancestor-worshipers in California. And they all had their theories, their own answers. I drank and roistered in the barrel-houses, the cribs, and the blind pigs of the dirty little towns along the Mexican border, and the people there had answers, too. And I listened to them all. But none of the answers seemed to be for me.

"And then one morning, outside of Pueblo, Colorado—" I paused, remembering.

"Go on," Gloria said.

I looked at her. Her expression was serious, interested. "You asked for it. All right. There were eight of us, maybe ten, waiting to shag the westbound freight. We were lying around beside a stream in a grove of cottonwoods in a hollow down a short hill from the roadbed.

"There was one kid along, a little Mexican kid—twelve, maybe thirteen years old. One of the men caught the kid trying to lift a pack of butts off him. This character and his pals gave the little Mexican a going-over. They roughed him up pretty well. It was none of my business. One thing you learn on the road, you learn that what anybody else does is none of your business. Unless they do it to you. That way you stay out of trouble.

"There was a little old man squatting beside me. He hadn't said a word since we'd been there. He was dirty and he stank. He had a scraggly little beard and that white stuff in the corners of his eyes, and his teeth, what there were of them, were dirty brown stumps.

"The man who owned the cigarettes finally drew a jackknife with a five-inch blade. The Mexican kid was lying on the ground moaning. The man with the jackknife grinned and the grin was ugly, and he said, 'We'll nut him. We'll nut the thieving little bastard. Somebody pull his pants down and we'll make a permanent soprano out of the little bastard!'

"I'm pretty sure he wouldn't have cut the kid, but he was scaring him plenty. The kid started screaming for mercy. The seedy little old man beside me stood up.

"He shouted in a thin voice, 'Lay off that kid!'

"The men around the kid laughed at the old man.

"The old man walked toward them. 'Get on away from that kid!' he said. His voice was quaking.

"'Go on,' the man with the knife told his pals. 'Get his pants down. I'm going to caponize the hell out of this here Mexican gamecock.'

"The old man kept right on walking. 'Leave him be!' he said.

"The character with the knife got a little upset. 'Stay the hell out of this, old man,' he said.

"The old man went right up to the man with the knife, who was twice his size. 'What are you, some kind of a goddamn jocker?' he asked the old man, and be gave him a cuff on the side of his head that knocked him down. The old man struggled to his feet. He was knocked down three times. Each time he stood right up for more.

"The third time he got to his feet this guy waved his knife at him. The old man walked straight toward him. 'Stand away from that kid!' he said. And this time, for some reason, his voice was no longer shaky—it was strong and firm.

"The man with the knife stood there with his mouth gaping. He started to speak, and no words came. He closed his knife and fumbled it into his pocket. He just stood there, his mouth open, staring at the old man. All of a sudden he started sidling away from the kid. His friends stood there gaping at the old man and then they, too, left the kid.

"That little old man knelt beside the kid and picked him up. He carried him to the bank of the stream and laid him down. He stroked the kid's matted hair from his forehead and bathed the blood from his face. Then the old man stood and turned toward me, and a shaft of sunlight shone through the branches of the cottonwood above him and caught him full in the face. I couldn't believe what I saw. Somehow the old man's eyes had cleared. Somehow that beard was no longer scraggly. He smiled, and his teeth shone strong and white in the sunshine. I looked into that face and I saw thousands of years of suffering and wisdom and kindness, and sympathy. That face was right out of the stained-glass window of some old cathedral.

"I started toward him. Just then the westbound freight pulled around the curve, with a lonesome sounding highball. Everybody but the Mexican kid and the old man and I started scrambling up the hill to shag it. I stood there for a moment watching the guys climb aboard. Then I turned around. The kid was there, but the old man had gone. The old man had *disappeared*, Gloria. I asked the kid where he was. All I got was a stupid stare. I grabbed his shoulders and shook him, and shouted at him: 'Where is he! Where's the old man?'

"The kid stared at me. 'Old man? What old man?'

"And I never saw him again."

Gloria was silent.

"What do you think? Was I dreaming?"

"I don't know," she said slowly. "Maybe it *was* some kind of miracle. Or maybe you only imagined the changes in the old man. But I know this: Only a kind man, a compassionate man, could even *think* he saw a thing like that."

Just then I couldn't even look at her. *How wrong*, I thought, *could a woman be?* And what would she think of me if she knew I was part and parcel of as dirty a little racket as I'd ever seen? How could she know that any kindness and compassion I might ever have had had started disintegrating in the sweating jungles of Guadalcanal, and had continued its dissolution in the filth of Stalag Number XI, and had received its death blow one night on a studio couch in an apartment on Fortieth Street in New York, and had been completely finished off in a ditch on a torn and bloody peninsula surrounded by the Yellow Sea and the Sea of Japan. How wrong could a woman be?

And then her cheek was next to mine, and she was in my arms again, and I felt embraced, caught up in the warmth rising from the rich soil. The air was sweet and heavy with the rich scent of things that grow too fast, too lushly. The same urgency was in us, but this time there was tenderness too. At the end the ferns around us seemed to explode in burning colors. And then Gloria was staring at me, her lovely eyes half fearful, half wondering. She raised a hand and slowly, tentatively, caressed the line of my jaw. Then suddenly she sighed. And with the sigh, the shadows passed from her eyes. She started to speak, then clung to me as if she would never let me go as I hushed her lovely mouth with a kiss.

Chapter Six

The place known simply as Adele's was eighteen miles from Cartersville, and the last eight or ten miles of the eighteen were over a rutted clay road. Adele's was situated in this inaccessible spot for obvious reasons. No casually cruising wife or mother or fiancée could possibly blunder onto her husband's or son's or her husband-to-be's car at Adele's. To begin with, she couldn't get by the guard at the gate at the head of the clay road. Nobody could, unless he was known or unless he had a letter from Adele, Rand Ringo, or one of the regulars. And the only women who had ever passed through that gate were Adele and the girls who worked for her.

The area around Adele's was a hunting preserve. It was leased by a group of men headed by Rand Ringo, and included several sportsmen from up North whom no one had ever seen and who may or may not have been actual persons. It was a hunting preserve, all right, because there was a sign over the heavy gate at the entrance that read SEMINOLE ROD AND GUN CLUB. PRIVATE—KEEP OUT! and the whole area was heavily fenced.

Adele and her girls had entertained some pretty important people, it was said. Some pretty influential men in the state—friends of Ringo's—and on one occasion even a governor of the state. Not that Ringo kept the place there just to entertain his friends. It was there to make money. And make money it did. Adele was a good madam. You couldn't find prettier girls in any similar establishment in the state. Or cleaner or more versatile ones. And Adele—just like a good football coach—was usually able to field a well-rounded team, with specialists in the various departments. It was said that quite a few wealthy men—from as far north as Tampa and as far south as Miami—had sent their sons, in their sixteenth or seventeenth years, to get their basic instruction in the gentle art of fornication from Adele and her girls.

It was strictly a man's world out there at Adele's. Nobody ever bothered you. There was a poker game in one of the back rooms of the main building that went on almost without cessation. There was a well-run bar in the main building. There were boats and motors and fishing equipment at the dock on the lake behind the establishment. There was a steam room for sweating out hangovers and a giant Negro masseur with hands like Georgia hams, to knead a man back into shape. Nobody seemed to care whether a man took a girl or not: they were simply there for his pleasure if he wanted them.

It was a man's world, all right. A great place to escape the sharp tongue of a nagging wife or the tight-lipped displeasure of a frigid one. A wonderful place to go on a week's drunk if the cares of the world had suddenly become too great. Adele's rates were high—much higher than the other places of its kind in the section—but nobody had ever been cheated or rolled at Adele's. A man could drink as much as he wanted to, as long as he didn't start any trouble, and Adele would see that he was put to bed when he passed out, washed when he became filthy, puked when he'd had more than he could hold, fed when he was hungry, steamed out, massaged, and taken home when his binge was done—if he was too shaky to drive his own car—in as respectable a condition as could be expected.

Adele's enjoyed a wonderful reputation. One of the girls had, it was true, made some pretty hysterical statements to the young new editor of the *Cartersville*

Weekly Herald several years back. And the young new editor had printed these statements in the *Herald*. This girl said that she and the rest of the girls were held in virtual slavery at Adele's. She said that they were beaten by the giant Negro masseur when they incurred Adele's displeasure by balking at some of her special instructions. She said that Adele had made heroin available to her girls and that several of them—herself included—had become addicts. And that all the money these girls made went right back to Adele for the H. And that most of the girls who had become addicts were afraid to leave their source of supply.

And she went on to tell the editor that one girl had become pregnant and had refused to deal with the abortionist that Adele had out from time to time, and that Adele had had her beaten and the girl had lost her baby and had died. The girl who was making the statements said that as far as she or any of the other girls knew, the girl who had died had simply been taken out in the scrub and buried.

The young new editor left town the day after these statements appeared in the *Herald*. Nobody seemed to know where he'd gone. Three days later the girl who'd done the talking was adjudged insane by the Carter County court and committed to the state asylum at Chattahoochee. There was a smattering of indignant talk around the county for a while but it soon died down. Who would believe a whore, anyway? And especially a drug-crazed whore?

But Ringo wasn't especially satisfied with the way things were going at Adele's. "Call it a routine checkup, perhaps," he said to me. "Call it anything you'd like. But there's something going on out there that I want to know about. For one thing, Adele's been drinking a lot lately. And the receipts are 'way off. But these things are minor. I've been informed that a couple of the Dade County boys have been seen sucking around out there recently. As I've told you, there's nothing that Dade County outfit would love better than to move in on me. I'm not intimating that Adele would be stupid enough to pull a fast one. But I have to know what's going on. She doesn't know you. Go out and see what you can find out." He wrote me a note that would get me through the gate.

It was a pleasant spot, built along the order of some beach and mountain resorts I had seen. There was a two-storied main building and a dozen individual cottages, or cabins, spaced far enough apart to insure complete privacy. All the buildings were constructed of unfinished pine plankings, giving the whole place a rustic effect.

I went into the main building. There was a desk in the small entrance hall and I was asked to register. Ringo had thought I might operate better under an assumed name. Adele had never seen me but she might have heard of me. He'd called me Danton in the note I'd given the gatekeeper. I registered as such. The pimply desk clerk asked me if I planned to spend the night and I told him I did. He assigned me to a cabin. I took the key, stowed my gear in the cabin he'd given me, and went back to the main building to look it over.

Half of the downstairs was living room. There was a bar in a small room off the dining room. Down a hall past the bar were a few private rooms equipped with chairs and tables—for private gatherings, poker, business conferences, I supposed. The girls and Adele lived upstairs.

The sun was setting and it was time for a drink. Two couples shared a booth opposite one end of the bar. I sat at a stool at the other end of the bar and ordered Old Forester and water from the colored barkeeper. A girl came in, sat at the other end of the short bar, and ordered a rum and coke. She was a pretty little thing—dark, very shapely, with smoldering, resentful eyes and a mouth that was a brilliant slash against a dead-white face. I signaled the bartender that the rum and coke was mine. He nodded, made the drink and gave it to her, whispered to her—and she came down to my end of the bar.

"All right, good-looking," she said. "Thanks."

"The pleasure is mine," I said.

Her eyes smoldered even more and her mouth went petulant. "You don't have to hand me that crap," she said.

"I mean it."

"You don't have to work anything up around here, good-looking. It's all ready to go." She gulped her drink.

I gave her a cigarette, took one myself, and lit them both.

"You want to go upstairs, good-looking?"

I grinned at her. "Don't rush me."

"You spending the night at this joint?"

I nodded.

"Ask for me if you want me. Virgie Lupfers."

"I'll keep you in mind, Virgie."

"I can give you anything the rest of these bags can give you."

I didn't say anything—just looked at her.

"Tell me this, good-looking," she said. "What's a man with a face and a build like you got doing in a cathouse?"

"Maybe I just happen to like cathouses."

"Don't hand me that. Nobody likes to pay for something they can get for free. Most of the men come to see us girls, they're either too fat or too old or too ugly to get it without buying it. Either that, or they haven't got guts enough to try. Or they're some kind of queers that want something special."

Her glass was empty. I ordered her another. "You forget one thing," I said. "A joint like this is the only place a man can have his fun and not worry about complications. Women are a possessive lot, you know, honey. When they've given a man what they consider their all—they usually start thinking they own him. There's not much hypocrisy in a whorehouse. A basic need is recognized as such and dealt with as such. This is the only country in the world where a man can drive a car when he's sixteen, fight a war when he's eighteen, but cannot—according to law and the generally accepted morals of the country—normally satisfy his sex needs until he's old enough to support a wife."

"You're over my head there, mostly," she said. "But you started out there talking about women. How do you think we girls feel about men? How do you think we get to feel about their soft bellies and their fat necks and their bald heads and their greedy hands and their hot pig eyes and their cigar-and-bourbon-stinking breaths and their slobbering mouths and the way they hate us when they're through with us?"

"Take it easy, kid. Relax. You'll live longer."

Her hand shook as she gulped down the rest of her rum and coke. I ordered her another one.

"My God, yes," Virgie said. "Sometimes I get all wound up, and things start churning around inside, like broken gears. Usually between the second and the third drink—after that it's all right." She stared into space for a minute. Then she looked at me sidewise. "Adele heard me talking to a customer like that, I'd be up the creek without a paddle. And I sure wasn't talking about you, good-looking."

"Forget it," I said. "You've been working too hard." I grinned at her. "What you need is a vacation. How'd you like to fly down to Havana with me for a week-end sometime?"

"You mean it?"

"Sure."

She looked as if she was about to cry then, and I suddenly realized how very young she was. "Adele wouldn't let me go."

"Does she own you?"

Her eyes were mournful. "Would you believe me if I said she did?"

I shrugged. "I want to meet Adele, anyway. I've heard a lot about her. Maybe I'll speak to her about that little trip." I hated to lie to her but this seemed like a good method of acquiring a personal introduction to the Queen Mother.

Her face brightened. "No stuff, good-looking?"

"No stuff," I said.

"Adele don't come down much anymore. She's been sick, or something. Nobody's seen much of her lately, not counting this big old lard-assed sheriff, Loy Bailey. Ugly? Boy, he's ugly! He was to fall in the lake there, they'd be skimming ugly off the surface for weeks! Old Loy sucks around here lots. Him and Adele sit up there in her place and talk and argue for hours. You can hear them sometimes in the hall."

It might be a lead, I thought. I played it slow and easy. "Yeah? Funny place for a sheriff to hang out."

She giggled. "Maybe he's in love."

I grinned at her. "Hogs mate. But they don't fall in love."

"He sure does suck around up there."

"He's not here now, is he?"

"I haven't seen him in a couple of days."

"You say you've heard them talking?"

"Mainly arguing."

"What about?"

She stared at me. "You're sort of curious, ain't you?"

"Forget it. Have another drink."

Her face softened. "Sure. And forget what I just said, good-looking. I don't mind telling you what they argue about. Just this and that. It don't make sense anyway. Things about bolita and bootlegging, just for instance. How the rackets should be run. I don't know exactly what. Like I said, it don't make sense. Adele don't sell bolita and this whisky ain't bootleg. Adele's got a club license." Virgie's voice sounded proud. "Just like a country club. Real high class."

I ordered another rum and coke for her. "Hear anything else?"

She grabbed for her drink. "Oh, they had a dandy here a week or so ago. Adele must have been drunk. I never have heard her roar and rant so. I like to have felt sorry for poor old Loy, and him trying to shush her up. 'Ringo,' she kept screaming. 'Ringo! All I hear is Ringo! When are you going to get the lead out of that big fat ass of yours? When are you going to do something?' Boy, she was screaming some! It was all poor old Loy could do to finally shush her."

She stared at her drink for a moment and then she looked up at me. "I been talking too much. Not that any of that shouting made any sense, but I still been talking too much. Adele heard me talking like *that* to you, I'd *really* be up that creek!"

I grinned at her. I had my lead. And if it went where I thought it went it would finish Loy Bailey. Cream him. And that was my happy thought for the day.

"Let's go meet Adele," I said.

She stood up. "You leave this rum and coke right here, Johnny. Hear?" she told the bartender.

The barkeep nodded and Virgie and I went upstairs. In the dark upstairs hall she stopped suddenly, wheeled, and threw herself against me, her thighs hard against mine. Her fingers dug into my shoulders. "Don't forget now, good-looking. You want me tonight, I'll be waiting. You just ask for me. Virgie. Virgie Lupfers."

Adele must have been, at one time, a very beautiful woman. Take away the hardness, now, and the puffiness around her eyes and the blatancy of her hennaed hair, and she still wasn't bad. She could have passed as a fairly hard-living club woman of forty-two or -three in any suburban society. Her figure was slim and trim in a tailored suit. She had met us at the door of her apartment and she had asked me in. Virgie hadn't been included. There was nothing whorehouse about the living room of Adele's apartment. It was severe—almost cold. I had been introduced by Virgie simply as her friend. Adele waved her hand toward the portable bar in a corner of the living room. She seemed fairly drunk.

"You do the honors, please, Mr—"

"Danton, ma'am. What shall I make you?"

"Martini, please. Six to one. And no more 'Ma'ams,' please. Ma'am is a contraction of madam and I don't care for the ugly connotation. I like to think of this place as a resort and of myself as supervisor of recreation." She giggled. A giggle was an incongruous sound in that severe room. I busied myself at the bar. The remains of a Martini were in the cocktail shaker. I poured them out and built a new one. A solitary gin drinker, I thought. Bad. I made myself a bourbon and water and poured her Martini. I had no idea in which direction to lead the conversation. I had decided to let her cue me. Virgie had given me a lead but I didn't want to use it until I had to.

"Please sit down, Mr. Danton."

I sat in a chair and she arranged herself, a little unsteadily, on a davenport.

"You've come to find out about Virgie Lupfers?"

That was as good as anything. I nodded.

"I admire a man who wants to know what he's buying. It proves that he's smart, discriminating. So many of my customers have no taste, no real appreciation. They come here for one thing and they're not particular how they get it—nor from whom—as long as they get it in a hurry. About Virgie. I think you'll like Virgie. She's quite young—she came to me two years ago when she was sixteen—young, but very passionate. And she has a lovely, firm young body. Perhaps you'd like to see her. *En déshabillé*, shall we say? I can get her back in a moment." Adele's voice had gone hard, flat. "It's a lovely young body, really—"

"That won't be necessary," I said.

She sounded disappointed. "As you say, Mr. Danton." She waved the empty glass at me unsteadily. "Would you, please?" I took the empty shaker and went to the bar. "Perhaps some of the other girls? I have a new girl in from Havana. Most versatile—"

"You've recommended Virgie. That's good enough for me." I'd decided to try a little flattery. I'd never seen a woman yet who wasn't susceptible to it—though I'd never tried it on a whorehouse madam before. "You've got a pretty fine reputation, Adele." I filled her glass. "I've always heard that you ran the best place in the state."

"Thank you," she said.

"I mean it."

She narrowed her eyes at me. Her voice was thick, her words slurred. "Are you trying to tell me something, Mr. Danton?"

I grinned at her. "No. Except that with a talent like yours I'm surprised to find you involved in an operation as small as this one."

I'd hit some kind of pay dirt with that. Adele went tense, catlike. "Did you come to see me to talk about that girl?"

I was groping in the dark. "Maybe."

"Where are you from, Mr. Danton?"

"Around."

"Such as where?"

"Such as Miami Beach, for one place."

"And such as Chicago, for another place?"

"Perhaps." I was flying blind. But I was remembering Ringo's statement about the Dade County boys and how they would love to move in on him. Maybe I could stir up something important here if I played it close to my vest and let Adele cue me. She was drunk enough, I felt, to talk.

"Goddamn it, Danton, say what you came here to say!"

"I'm just making conversation, Adele. I'm simply saying that you could go places with the right connections. This could be a real uptown joint with the right backing. No more of this small-time, chicken—"

That did it. Her eyes flashed. "I don't know who sent you here, Danton. But I can find out. And I've got a pretty good idea who it was, anyhow! And I'll tell you the same thing I told the other two mugs that were hanging around here last week! You go back to your people in Miami Beach and tell them that Adele is doing all right! Small time! Let me tell you something, mister. Adele has never been small time in her life!"

She stopped yelling at me long enough to knock off what was left of the Martini I'd just poured her. Her face was drawn and ugly as she stood unsteadily and wiped gin from her chin with the back of her hand. "You're so high and mighty, you people! I've been around. I know what happens to people who play footsie with you Chicago-Miami Beach hoods. I know who gets the dirty end of the stick!"

She took a deep breath and sat down. Her lips clamped together and I figured she was through talking. I had found out exactly nothing—except that Adele didn't care for the boys from Dade County. On the other hand, perhaps she was playing hard to get. Waiting. If she was leveling with Ringo, why hadn't she told him that the boys from down the state were making passes at her? If I wasn't adding two and two and getting five, then she and Loy Bailey had plans for knocking over Ringo. Or *she* had plans and was trying to sell them to Loy. The arguments between them that Virgie had overheard could mean little else. I didn't think that Loy Bailey had ever had an idea in his life. But this woman Adele was a pretty cold fish. And ambitious—even if she did drink too many Martinis. I'd have bet ten bucks against a plugged nickel that she'd been trying to sell Bailey the idea that *he'd* run this county if Ringo were out of the way. And that was good for a belly laugh. But I didn't exactly feel like laughing. Ringo had sent me here for information. And so far all I had was ideas. But they were pretty important ideas. Important to me, personally. If they went gunning for Ringo they'd want me out of the way first.

I said softly, "Now don't get upset again, Adele. It's bad for your stomach. Just relax and hear me out. The man down there is a sportsman. A regular Abercrombie and Fitch sort of a guy. You know, very high class. Likes everything real nice. He's interested in acquiring a hunting preserve in this county. This one, or one just like it, with you running it. There's a rumble around that you might be interested in a deal. *Later*, that is."

Her eyes were wary. "What do you mean—*later?*"

I shrugged.

"I don't know what you mean by *later*," she insisted.

I grinned at her. "You're pretty friendly with a man named Loy Bailey, aren't you, Adele? Sheriff Loy Bailey?"

A shadow of fear flicked across her eyes.

"Maybe I ought to talk to Bailey."

"Him!" she shouted. "That stupid bastard! Listen, mister, I'm the one who'll be—" She choked it off with an ugly, gurgling sound. "Get out of here! Hit the road, you cheap hood!"

"Yes, ma'am," I said. I got up.

"Goddamn you!" she screamed. "I told you not to call me that!"

I shook my head. "Women's vanity," I said. "Thanks, Adele. It's been charming. And highly instructive."

She was heading for the Martini pitcher when I left her. Whether to throw it at me or build another drink

I didn't know. But I would have bet on the former. There was no doubt in my mind that she and Bailey had plans to take over the county. And Adele was smart enough to know what I was thinking. And when she'd called the gatekeeper to check on me, when she'd found out that my note was from Ringo, my life wouldn't be worth much around this particular health resort. I rigged a quick excuse for the desk clerk, paid my bill, and went to my cabin for my bag. Virgie was there, in a sheer black nightgown—ready to go to work. I told her I had to leave. "Take me with you. For God's sake take me with you!"

I wrenched her arms from around my neck.

Now she was sobbing. "Please. Please take me with you!"

"I'm sorry, kid," I said. I hated to leave her but I had it to do. Adele was a fast worker. As I passed the corner of the cabin on my way to my car I felt a gun shoved against my back and I could smell the stink of stale sweat.

If I had waited even a second it would probably have been too late. My bag was in my right hand. I whirled to the right and pounded the gun arm away from the small of my back with the bag. The gun flashed and roared as the round kicked up dirt at my feet. I dropped the bag and crossed a hard left to the man's stomach. The stomach was soft and I heard him gasp and I knew that this was the place to work him over. I saw the gun barrel coming in time to duck under it and I was inside the flailing arms and then I really went to work. In the dark I couldn't see much, but I knew the man was huge and I knew he was black and I figured him to be Adele's masseur and hatchet man. And I knew that if I couldn't finish him off by working his soft belly over, I was all through.

I'd gotten to his breath now and he started sinking to his knees, gasping, retching. He dropped the gun and I grappled for it in the dirt with a free hand, found it, and brought the butt of it hard against the side of his head. He slumped to the ground.

I caught a last glimpse of Virgie standing in the open doorway of the cabin staring at the Negro, her eyes wide with terror, and my wheels spun in the sand as I shoved my Ford into gear and roared out of there.

Chapter Seven

The information I had was red hot. I knew that I should pass it along to Ringo. After all—I'd taken the man's money. He had trusted me. I owed him that much. And besides that, my life wasn't worth much as long as Loy Bailey was around. Adele would certainly tell him that I knew too much. She'd describe me to him and he'd peg me immediately. And that didn't make me a good insurance risk. But I was greedy. I had information that would blow this organization sky-high. And I tried to figure how to use it best to my own advantage. I decided to sit on it for a few days, be extremely careful, and see what happened.

When I reported to Ringo I told him I'd talked with Adele, that she'd been on a booze kick, all right—but that he didn't have a thing to worry about as far as her playing ball with the Dade County boys. I told him I'd represented myself to her as one of them and that I'd been told off in no uncertain terms. He seemed satisfied. As a matter of fact, he asked me on an outing.

"I've got a fishing lodge down the river, Dolan," he said. "My wife and my daughter and I are going down for Saturday and Sunday. I'd like to have you join us."

"Sounds good to me." I had to be polite.

"How long has it been since you've seen a cockfight?"

"Quite a while," I said. As a matter of fact I'd raised them, pitted them, and handled them myself when I was a high-school kid back in West Virginia. And I'd spent a little time around the pits in Mexico City.

"Like them?"

"I can take them or leave them."

"Great sport. Gamest thing alive, a fighting cock. All heart. I raise them and fight them in mains and hacks and derbies all over the southeast. Allen Roundheads—that's my breed. My cocks won better than twenty thousand dollars for me at the Internationals at Orlando last year. I have a pit at my place down the river. We're running an eight-cock derby down there on Sunday afternoon. The best of my pit stock will be there."

"I'll be looking forward to it."

"Be here at noon on Saturday, then."

Gloria and Billy had gone when I arrived at Ringo's on Saturday; they were making the trip down the river in Gloria's speedboat. Ringo and I made the trip in my Ford. Ringo's lodge—a forty-minute drive over back roads from Cartersville—was an old Florida frame house that he had bought and rehabilitated. He'd added a screened porch that stretched the width of the house, and he'd knocked away walls to make a big living room. The bedrooms were upstairs. A dock— pocked and chewed by buckshot where Ringo and previous inhabitants had killed moccasins sleeping in the sun—was directly in front of the screened porch: the door from the porch opened onto it. Between two and three hundred yards behind the house, in a grove of live oaks, was Ringo's cockpit, roofed against the weather, with bleacher seats to accommodate perhaps a hundred people ringing the pit. Quite an establishment. I wondered aloud why anyone had built a house like this, originally, in this out-of-the-way spot.

Ringo smiled. "We're not too far from the big lake here, Dolan. And in the twenties this country was pretty wild. Not much law around Okeechobee in those days—and little enough now. This house was sort of a clearing station. Wasn't too much of a trick to bring the stuff over from Bimini to Stuart, through the St. Lucie Canal, across the lake, and dump it here. If government taxes on the stuff go much higher it might still be good. You've heard of the Ashley gang? John Ashley, his brothers, and the rest of them? The boys who tried to run a road block outside of Fort Pierce and were cut down and slaughtered when they showed fight?"

I nodded, thinking that John Ashley had been a piker compared to Rand Ringo. Ashley and his boys had simply been bank robbers, booze runners, and hijackers.

"A brave man, Ashley," Ringo said. "The closest thing to legend—in the Jesse James, Dalton Brothers, Billy the Kid tradition—that we have in these parts. I was a kid in my teens when Ashley was operating up and down the lower east coast and hiding out in the 'Glades. 'King of the Everglades,' the papers used to call him. I remember crying my eyes out when they killed him. He was a man, Dolan. An individualist. He laughed at them all, threw his courage in their faces."

He stared at me as he said this, his eyes sad, lonely—and for a moment I felt sorry for the man. From time to time, I'd noticed, his face went naked and he seemed lost, crying out for reassurance. I didn't have the heart just then to remind him that Ashley had been a stupid, illiterate hood who, when he had died face down on a highway with a belly full of lead, had gotten exactly what he deserved.

"John Ashley unloaded plenty of booze at this dock. This was a great spot for live cargo, too. Chinese in from Havana, around the Keys, inside the Tortugas, through the Ten Thousand Islands to Fort Myers. Then up the Caloosahatchee and across the lake to the Kissimmee. Rugged characters, those live-cargo runners. Reckless. They knew what they were after and they took all sorts of chances to get it!"

Ringo's eyes were shining now; as always when he was excited, his hands clenched into powerful fists.

"Around the Keys it was always dangerous for them. Very tricky. Coast Guard cutters. You know what they'd do, Dolan, when they were in close waters?" His voice was tense with excitement. "They kept fifty-gallon oil drums aboard their boats. The drums were all rigged to a line that was made fast to the stern of the boat. When the going became real tricky they'd load the Chinamen two to a drum and put the drums overboard. A man stood by in the stern sheets with an ax. If the Coast Guard hailed them he cut the line. If they were boarded, the evidence was gone. How's that for being cool? How's that for ingenuity?"

"What about the Chinese?"

"If the cutter left them alone, they'd go back later. If they were lucky, they'd find a few."

"A little rough on the Chinese."

"They took their chances. Some of them would drift ashore onto the Keys or the mangrove islands. If the mosquitoes didn't kill them, if they didn't starve or die of thirst, they had a chance of making it to civilization. A few Chinese more or less wouldn't make much difference. Ever hear of James Horace Alderman, who was hanged at Fort Lauderdale? The greatest alien runner of them all. He's dropped hundreds of Chinese right here. Right on this dock!"

"Interesting," I said. "But don't you have any heroes who died in bed?"

His mouth went pouty, like some great child's. He hated being kidded, even a little bit. "I'm going upstairs and relax for a while. Ask the boy in the kitchen for anything you want. The girls won't be in for a couple of hours."

I looked in the boathouse at the far end of the dock. Two skiffs, with outboards, were slung on hoists. I lowered one—a sixteen foot Lyman with a 25-h.p. Evinrude on its tail. I checked the two tanks, found them full, cranked up, swung clear of the boathouse, and started down river. The river coiled and writhed like a snake, and I knew then why Gloria and Billy were still on their way. Ten miles by water must have moved me a mile as the pond birds flew it.

It was a wild and a beautiful country. Egrets, limpkins, coot, and birds of a hundred varieties took off in shrieking clouds as I rounded the turns. Alligators, some of them almost as long as my boat, dozed on the mud flats on the inside of the turns and scuttled for the river—surprisingly fast—as the nose of my boat poked into view. I had been told that they moved faster on land—for the first ten or fifteen yards—than a dog or a pig. Until I had seen them flash from the mud banks to the river I hadn't believed it.

The hot afternoon sun nursed me into a state of half-awareness, of idly meandering thoughts. And—as always—they drifted to Dusty Randall. I'd often wondered why. Was it because a man could never completely get over his first real love? Or was it due to some suppressed masochistic urge? I thought of Dusty—Dusty as I had first known her, with her flair for living, her insatiable curiosity about people. She'd always loved talking and listening to all sorts of people, all sorts of characters. Old men feeding pigeons in Central Park and soapbox orators in Union Square and hustlers in little joints off Broadway and crackpots and screwballs in Third Avenue bars.

I remembered the evening we'd spent dissecting a dozen isms over bad whiskey in a smoky Village walk-up with five or six of Dusty's more artistic friends. If I remembered correctly, there was a painter who wouldn't show anybody his canvases, a writer who despised the *Saturday Evening Post* and claimed a spiritual affinity with Rainer Maria Rilke, and a fervent young theatrical producer who thought the only decent thing done on the American stage since *The Cherry Orchard* had been the little thing he'd staged at the summer theater at Sag Harbor, in which the only stage property was a tree, and the three members of the cast were apes, appropriately done up in ape suits from Brooks Costumes.

And then there was an actor with the ungodly name of Oscar Gramercy. Gramercy was wearing an unpressed suit. His necktie was flying at half-mast. His face, sad, thin, fey, was pure Irish poet—and Dusty was fascinated by him.

"What's with you, Gramercy?" she asked him. "You've been introduced as an actor. What have you done?"

"Nothing. Not yet."

"You *should* be an actor. You've got an actor's face and an actor's voice. But where did you find that horrible name?"

His face lighted with pleasure and gratitude. "I am an actor, darling. I'm all actor! I'm no good for anything else. You know what happened to me?" He didn't wait for an answer. "My father is a powerhouse back home. He's big politics in my home state. I won't tell you his name because you've heard of him. He's an Irish politician. Besides being a politician he's a businessman on the side, see: state road commissioner, contracting firm on the side; state milk commissioner, dairy farm on the side. You know how it goes—dirty, lowdown. My father is a son of a bitch.

"He also owns a velvet mill. He wants me to learn the business and run it for him. Let me tell you something: I'd rather carry a beautiful goddamn shining spear for beautiful goddamn shining Katherine Cornell for the price of three meals a day in the Automat and a hall bedroom, than run, or even own, the biggest goddamn velvet mill in the world! Do you see what I mean?"

Dusty nodded eagerly.

"I call myself Oscar Gramercy because Oscar Gramercy is the purest goddamn most unmitigated ham actor name that I could think of. And one of these days I'm going to slap my old man in his dirty politicking puss with a fifty-foot neon sign all lit up with that lousy ham name!"

Dusty reached forward and touched his face, softly. "And you will, you will...."

And then for several months, until Dusty tired of him, Oscar Gramercy was our friend. And after Gramercy it was a trumpet player from one of the hot combos that worked the joints along Fifty-Second Street. And after the trumpet player a kid welterweight from Pittsburgh. These were our friends. Dusty liked them, and I played along. Always the quick people, the nervous and the odd people. And—until that night in the apartment on Fortieth Street—I never knew, never even suspected, that my wife was a tramp.

I shook my head to clear it of musty thoughts of the past. That was done and gone. I had plenty of thinking to do about the present. I wasn't looking forward to this week-end. I was here simply because an invitation from Ringo was an order. I didn't relish the idea of spending a night under the same roof with both Billy and Gloria—anything might happen. I'd have to be plenty cagey tonight and tomorrow, I knew. I'd make like the hired hand that I was and stay out of everybody's way as much as possible. It would be hard, though.

I took a couple of wrong turns going back—the river is full of forks and it's easy to go wrong—and it was late when I got in. The speedboat was there. Ringo, Gloria, and Billy were sitting in the big living room having drinks. I made my entrance as inconspicuously as possible. I had to tear my eyes away from Gloria; she was so beautiful that if I kept looking at her I knew I'd have to go to her, touch her, somehow.

"You've met my wife?" Ringo asked me.

"Yes."

"Of course you have. I'd forgotten. Billy's been asking for you. Haven't you, Billy?"

Billy's eyes were on her glass. She nodded.

"I said haven't you, Billy?" Ringo's tone was pleasant. He could have missed her nod, but I didn't think so for a moment. It sounded as if he was starting to give Billy a bad time. Did he know about us? Perhaps he suspected us and was simply trying to prove his suspicions.

It was possible, I thought, that he'd arranged this week-end to throw us together, see us squirm, like bugs under a microscope. He would enjoy that.

"Yes," Billy said.

"Why don't you make Dolan a drink, Billy?"

Billy started to get up. I stopped her. "I'll shower and change first. Sorry I'm late. I took a couple of wrong turns."

"That's easy for a man to do," Ringo said. "This river has killed a lot of people. We're still pretty raw around here, Dolan; civilization is only skin deep. It's dangerous to make mistakes around here, Dolan. Watch it."

So now he was starting in on me.

I stared at him, hating his smugness. If he had some sort of an idea that he was going to ride herd on me with a lot of innuendoes and double talk, he was wrong. If he tried to pin Billy's unfaithfulness on me I'd do everything I could to duck the rap. For Billy's sake, and mine, too. But I wouldn't squirm. And I wouldn't scare. He wouldn't run a sandy on me. I'd stay in the pot until I saw his hole card. "Thanks for the advice, Ringo. But I don't need it. I can take care of myself. Excuse me."

His lips twisted in a grimace of frustration as I left the room.

A hot shower relaxed me. Perhaps, I thought, I'd been dreaming this thing up. A guilty conscience can raise hell with a man's imagination. After all, Ringo had said nothing particularly offensive. Perhaps that crack of his about the river had been offered, and should have been taken, at face value. The guy was a ham, a real cornball. He loved to dramatize situations and he loved stage center. It was entirely possible that I was taking him too seriously. I got dressed, feeling happier about things.

Dinner—and a good one, too—was served by Ringo's combination cook, butler, and caretaker—a colored boy named Preacher. In spite of the well-prepared foods and the good wines, it was a painful forty-five minutes. Billy's face was flushed and her eyes were not quite focusing. Gloria ate, drank, spoke, and moved like a girl in a trance. She was gracious, she was polite, she answered intelligently when spoken to, but—with all her loveliness—she was a pale copy of the girl I had seen a few days before on that bluff overlooking the river. My stomach knotted as I fought down an unholy desire to stand up, slam my plate to the table, take her by the shoulders, and shake some life into her. Instead of that I made table talk with Ringo.

It was a relief to move back into the living room for coffee and brandy. Preacher brought the coffee service and the Hennessy 5-Star to a coffee table by Billy. Ringo stopped him.

"Better give that to Miss Gloria," he said. "I don't think Mrs. Ringo is quite up to it." When Preacher had left the room, Ringo said, "I don't know whether you've noticed it or not, Dolan—my wife drinks. Cigar?" He passed me a box of Havana panatelas. I took one and lighted it. So it was starting all over again. I didn't want to look at Billy just then.

Ringo moved across the room to the phonograph and put on a recording of Ravel's *Miroirs*.

"Great, isn't it, Dolan?" he said, after a while.

I listened for a moment longer. "A little theatrical, don't you think?"

His face reddened, his eyes flashed anger at me, and I was reminded again of some great spoiled child who was about to go into a tantrum because someone had crossed him. He took a couple of deep breaths and brought himself under control.

"Dolan, you're quite a guy. But I'll stump you yet." He turned to Billy. "What do you think of it, Billy?"

"I don't know." Billy's voice was toneless.

"She doesn't know, Dolan," Ringo said.

"I heard her," I said.

"Billy's a Harry James fan," Ringo said.

"So am I," I said. I glanced at Billy. She shot a grateful look at me.

Gloria said, "Coffee, Billy? Black?"

"Lace it with brandy, darling," Ringo said. "You know how she likes it."

"Mr. Dolan?" Gloria said.

"Black, please. And lace it with brandy."

I went to her for Billy's cup. As I took it my finger brushed hers and I watched her and for a moment her face seemed on the verge of coming to life. I took Billy's cup to her and her hand shook as she took it from me.

Ringo leaned against the mantle. "Well, what can we do for amusement?" he said. "Moonlight ride on the river? I guess you've had enough of the river for one day, you three. I don't think Billy's up to bridge—"

"We could pull the wings off flies," I said. I couldn't help it.

Ringo chose to disregard this. He sat on the arm of Gloria's chair and his fingers played with the ends of her shining mass of hair. "Not enough of us for charades, I suppose. And that's too bad. My wife was an actress, Dolan. Did you know that? A model and an actress. You can tell that by looking at her, can't you, Dolan?"

"Yes," I said.

"She had some amusing stories to tell about her career. I think Mr. Dolan would be interested, dear. You might have mutual friends. Mr. Dolan was married to a model. A beautiful girl. Dusty, her name was. Dusty—Dusty Randall. Isn't that right, Dolan?"

I heard Gloria stifle a hoarse, gasping sound, and I looked at her and her face had come alive for the first time that evening. She was staring at me and her eyes were warm with sympathy and concern. I was puzzled.

"Isn't it?" Ringo repeated. "Isn't it, Dolan?"

Why all the excitement, I wondered? "Yes," I said.

"They didn't get along." In his voice now there was a combination of mockery and amusement. Rather as if he, from some self-appointed Godlike elevation, was looking down and watching me twist in the mud of my own personal failure and finding it vastly amusing. He was watching me. I wanted to see him sprawling on the floor. I wanted to see that smugness ground into his face. *Don't do it, Dolan! Goddamn you, don't do it!*—and this time I heeded the warning.

I could sense his disappointment at his failure to get a rise out of me. He turned to Billy. "Go ahead, darling. Tell Mr. Dolan about your career."

Gloria stood up. "Excuse me. I—it's hot in here. I'm going for a walk." She hurried to the front door. I was aching to go with her but I knew I'd never get away with it.

"They wanted me to be in pictures—" Billy stared at me. I'd had a beagle bitch once when I was a kid. She'd turned up missing. I'd gone through the valley looking for her. I'd found her with one foot caught and mangled in a fox trap. I remembered her eyes as she had looked at me. Billy's eyes were like that now.

"They kept telling me I ought to be. I was going to have a screen test. They kept on saying—"

"You're being repetitive, darling," Ringo said.

I fought to keep my voice on a conversational level. "Why don't you let her tell her story, Ringo?"

She flashed me a look of pure gratitude. Then she faced Ringo and for the first time that evening she showed fight. I could have kissed her for it. "What do

you know about it?" she said. "What do you know
about anything but counting your money and hurting
people? I was good. Plenty good! And if I hadn't met
you I'd still be good!"

I glanced at Ringo. I was amazed to see the
combination of incredulity and hurt in his eyes, in the
set of his mouth.

Billy's voice was heavy with drunken pride. "I'll tell
Dolan how good I was. I'd love to tell Dolan how good
I was. Want to hear how good I was, Dolan?"

I nodded. I was beginning to feel a little ill.

"You take a lighthouse. You ever hear of a man so
crazy about a girl he wanted to give her a lighthouse?
Bet I'm the only girl in the whole wide world anybody
wanted to give a lighthouse to." She seemed to have
trouble focusing her eyes as she turned and faced
Ringo. "You, you chinchy bastard, I'll bet you never
offered to give a girl a lighthouse!"

"Go on with your story, Billy," Ringo said.

"Fella named Carl. Older fella. Crazy 'bout me.
Simply crazy. 'My God, Carl,' I told him, 'what would
I do with a lighthouse,' I said, and he said, 'Well, baby,
I just thought you might like it, but if it don't appeal
to you why don't you just go over to upper Broadway
and see my pal with the Buick agency instead. You
been driving that heap eight months now and no little
girl of mine should be seen driving a heap that old—'"

She stared at me. "You see what I mean, Dolan.
You see the possibilities there?"

"Yes," I said.

"Pour me some brandy, Dolan. I like brandy. It
makes my stomach warm and it reminds me of the way
things were. Good old brandy."

I glanced at Ringo. He nodded. I got the bottle and
filled a pony and took it to her.

She slopped a little of it as she took it from me. She
grinned drunkenly. "I saw you!" she said. "I saw you

look at him first! You're chicken, too—aren't you, Dolan? Old Chicken Dolan!"

I couldn't understand why Ringo didn't break it up. His wife, his house—and there was nothing I could do.

"Go ahead, darling." Ringo actually sounded pleased with himself.

"My 'Wild Irish Rose', Carl used to call me. Lived up in Boston, Carl did, and he'd come down to New York maybe once a month, and boy, we'd really live it up! Cub Room at the Stork—Carl and Mr. Billingsley were just like that—" She held up two fingers that she couldn't quite manage to bring together. "Twenty-One, Morocco, best seats at the best shows, Belmont, Jamaica—and you think Carl and I messed around with any two-dollar show tickets you're crazy, because it was a hundred bucks on the nose or at least across the board. A hundred bucks *anyhow!* Carl thought I had the most beautiful body and the loveliest face in the world, and he said I was going places, real high places, and he wanted to go along for the buggy ride, and if I wouldn't take him with me he'd kill himself."

She hiccupped, and tried dredging up a demure, apologetic-little-girl's sort of a smile that came out all crooked and messed up; it would have looked ridiculous anyway on her. She swallowed more brandy.

"Trouble with fur coats, when you model 'em, you model 'em in the summer, July or August, you know, so they can get the ads ready for fall. And this one day I was modeling fur coats in Central Park. For Pagano, I think—real nice guys there at Pagano's, they'd leave a girl alone, you know what I mean? And God it was hot, and I was bushed, and when I got home to my apartment in Tudor City—I was living in Tudor City, then, all by myself, except for Cheri, my French poodle—all I wanted was a little rest. Because the agent I had at the time had wangled two tickets to some sort of a publicity do—a movie thing—at the Ambassador.

Spencer Tracy and Katherine Hepburn were going to be there, and a whole lot of movie executives, too, and my agent insisted—really *insisted* that I go there with him, because this, he said, would probably be the one thing we needed to get us over the hump. And so who do you think was there? In my apartment? Who, Dolan?"

I wouldn't answer her. I had to sit there and listen to her tear herself apart but I didn't have to help her do it. I wondered why Ringo didn't beat her. It would have been cleaner. And quicker.

"Carl!" she said. "Well, I had to tell poor old Carl that, as much as I'd like to be with him that evening, my career came first. You've never *heard* a man carry on so. You'd have thought I'd kicked him in the stomach. He turned white, and then he started threatening me, accusing me of two-timing him, and I told him he'd better leave and not come back until he'd had time to think it over. When he saw he couldn't get anywhere threatening me, he started pleading with me. And then he started crying. Actually crying, blubbering! He said I was the only beautiful thing in his life. He got right down on his knees, right down on the floor, and he grabbed me around the knees and I could actually feel his tears on my legs. Really, actually, *feel* them! He begged me not to leave him that evening. Said he'd kill himself if I did!

"I'd never seen a man cry like that before, just like a baby, and I told him he was acting like a fool, and if that was the way he was going to act, like he owned me, and all, then we'd better just call it quits, I told him. Then I said my agent was practically positive we'd be landing that Hollywood contract soon, anyhow, and that we'd have to break it off sooner or later, anyhow, I told him."

She made two passes at her mouth with the pony glass and made contact the third time. She stared at me with anguished eyes and I just sat there and wished I were somewhere, anywhere, else.

She hiccupped again, then went on with her story: "He went away, Carl did, without saying anything else, and I went to the party at the Ambassador, all right. A lot of phonies and their babes were there, all free-loading, and I didn't even *see* Tracy and Hepburn, the way the joint was loused up with free-loaders, all telling stories about Moss Hart and Shirley Booth, and I might just as well have spent the evening with Carl.

"That agent! What a louse *he* turned out to be! Not even an office, only a hat! But I hung around the Ambassador till I got sick of it, and then I took a cab home. I picked up a late edition of the *Mirror* before I got in the cab and I was thumbing through it when we'd stop by lights, and on the third page I saw about Carl. 'Prominent New England Industrialist' it called him. He'd gone off the platform in the subway station at Columbus Circle and Broadway in front of an incoming train.

"The papers blamed it on financial reverses. Financial reverses! I could have told 'em. You bet your sweet life I could have told 'em. I could have told 'em I woke up screaming for months with my legs burning where his tears had run down 'em! I could have told 'em why he died!"

"That's very dramatic, darling," Ringo said.

"You shut up! You're so goddamn smug! I tell you I was good! They all wanted me. They kept on saying I ought to be in pictures. They—" And then the tears came, rasping, grating, and Ringo was beside her, helping her to her feet, and his voice sounded sincere as he said, "There, dear, there. You'll feel better in the morning."

And he led her from the room.

I sat there for a moment. Then I got up and walked out on the dock. Gloria was at the far end of it, staring out across the river. I went to her.

"Brad," she said softly, "was it bad?"

"It was bad."

"Brad, what am I going to do? I want to love him—and then I see what he does to her. And he enjoys it, Brad, I know he does. Why?"

There was a knot in my stomach that wouldn't go away, and I had a dirty taste in my mouth. I felt the same way I'd once felt when I'd seen an M.P. beat a wounded Jap P.O.W. and I had lacked the guts or the inclination to stop him. I didn't want to talk about it and I didn't want to think about it. I wanted to go to sleep and forget about it. It was no concern of mine.

"I don't know. Good night, Gloria."

Her face came alive then; her eyes burned into mine. "Brad!"

"Good night!"

When I got to my room I heard Ringo go back downstairs. I undressed and lay sweating on my bed and listened to the sobs coming from the room down the hall, and it was all I could do to keep from going down there and stopping them.

Chapter Eight

Billy didn't show up for the late breakfast the next morning. Gloria had eaten earlier and was on the river. Ringo and I finished breakfast and went to the cockpit. The crowd—dusty-eyed, sharp-cheeked cracker men for the most part, with a sprinkling of moon-faced, barrel-thighed women—had begun to gather. Pickup trucks with cooped cocks in their beds were parked under the live oaks. Handlers were walking cocks scheduled for the early pittings. Ringo walked among the men, with a slightly condescending lord-of-the-manor swagger, greeting the ones he knew. The men returned the greeting politely, but with no warmth. It was fairly obvious that they lost no love on Ringo.

Ringo's cocks had been brought up from Cartersville in a truck by a man introduced to me as Fee. Fee, it seemed, was an old-time cocker from Alabama. Ringo had found him there, down on his luck, and had brought him on to Cartersville to raise and handle his pit stock. Fee showed me the stock he'd brought for the day's pittings—likely looking Allen Roundheads, fit and aggressive. He saved the best until last:

"Right here's the boss-man's favorite," he said, "and well he should be. The finest, airiest gamecock in the Southeast, at least. Osceola, the boss-man calls him. He's a shake: he'll weigh in at about six pounds nine. He's a fighter, and mean to handle. Boss-man likes to pit him himself sometimes, and I hope he does today. I'll tell you the truth, Mr. Dolan, with two-and-a quarter inches of killing gaff strapped to each spur, I'm might proud when he does. This shake's been pitted nine times and he's yet to lose a fight."

"Fine-looking bird," I agreed.

I made the rounds, listening to the talk, sizing up cocks that looked like good bets. I found one man—a sharp-eyed, gnarly little old cracker with a squirrely way of moving—who had a truckload of chickens that caught my fancy. They were Pure Law Grays, and the Grays had been my favorites when I was raising gamecocks back in West Virginia. The little old man was trying to heel one of his cocks and he was having a tough time of it; one of his hands was heavily bandaged across the palm and he was cursing.

"Give you a hand, mister?" I said,

He narrowed his eyes at me.

"Hold him steady," I said. I was surprised how quickly it all came back to me. I wrapped the spurs quickly and neatly and I took the needle-pointed gaffs from their leather case and I fitted the leather bases of the gaffs over the spurs. Then I bound them firmly to

the cock's horny legs. The little man tested them. His
face warmed.

"Son, I'm mighty obliged to you."

I grinned at him. "Glad to give you a hand."

"A hand is just what I needed. Snagged this one on
a barbed wire fence three days ago. Thought nothing
of it until she started swelling up on me the middle of
last night. Had a man, a so-called friend of mine,
supposed to help, but the son of a bitch hasn't been
away from his old lady for a year, and he couldn't
stand freedom. Went juking last night and I haven't
seen worthless hide nor hair of him since."

"I'll be around to help you."

"Son, that's might nice of you. You're hired. O. D.
Bigelow's the name, from Tifton, Georgia."

"Dolan, O.D. And I'm doing it for fun."

"All right, son. I didn't mean to say you looked like
you needed an afternoon's work. Tell you what,
though—and keep this under your hat and the odds'll
stay right." He looked cautiously around him, then
lowered his voice. "See that shake there at the left of
the truck-bed?"

I nodded.

"That shake will go six pounds seven ounces, and
there ain't an ounce of fat on him. He's all heart and
pecker. He'll tread a yard full of chickens before a man
can set down for breakfast. And I'll stake my
reputation as a gamecock man if that shake there ain't
the highest-breaking, deadliest-cutting, smartest-
stepping bird in this derby. He's young, yet, and he
hasn't had much experience, but I know a good thing
when I get holt of it, and this bird and I are going
places. He's trained down fine and ready to go. For a
month now I've fed him corn, wheat, oats, and
buckwheat to strengthen him. He's had raw meat and
oysters to make him mean, and greens to freshen him.
He's been worked daily on the running board and the
flirting table and he's sparred twice a day. If that bird

ain't ready I'm a suck-egg mule. You want me to tell you something, well, get your money down on this Gray shake when I'm ready to pit him."

"What's he paired with?"

"I don't know for sure. Being a shake, he'll fight at catch weights. They haven't finished the pairings yet."

"What if he draws Ringo's Osceola?"

"Let him. I got a mighty strong feeling I got something here can whip anything that high and mighty son of a bitch can pit!" Bigelow took the Gray I'd just heeled under his arm and started for the pit.

The first fight had started while I was heeling Bigelow's cock. A Pierce Shuffler and a Blue Red had gone beak-to-beak, with the Shuffler showing just enough fight to break the long count, and they had been moved to the drag pit for the kill. Bigelow's Gray weighed in at 5:5 and was matched with a Warhorse of the same weight in the next fight.

I sat in the bleachers. The bets were conservative—ten, twenty, or thirty dollars—and I knew they'd get bigger as the excitement rose and the bottles made their rounds. Even money was being offered on this match by the Warhorse's supporters and I raised a hand and closed a bet with a man across the pit who wanted twenty dollars on the Warhorse.

Bigelow and the Warhorse's handler were billing their cocks.

"Ready," the referee called.

The two men got their cocks on the ground. "Pit!"

The men released them and stepped back behind their scores.

It was the quickest twenty dollars I ever made. The split second Bigelow released his cock the Gray flew straight for the Warhorse. He caught him on his score and gave one long rolling shuffle that sounded like taking the slack out of a freight train.

"Handle!" the referee called.

One of the Gray's heels was in the Warhorse's breast to its socket. The Warhorse's handler gently removed it. The referee's call to pit was a formality. The Gray shuffled once on the dead Warhorse and was declared the winner.

I bet them as I saw them from then on—playing no favorites. The bets, as I had known they would, got higher as time went on. I won three more bets, averaging better than a hundred a bet, on Bigelow's grays. I collected a three-hundred-dollar bet on one of Ringo's Roundheads. I lost a hundred and fifty on two of Bigelow's Grays and a hundred on one of Ringo's Roundheads. I won a couple of hundred on a Pure Law Clipper that had looked good to me. And in the meantime I was taking time out to heel all of Bigelow's Grays for him. The old man's injured hand was getting no better, and his eyes and cheeks looked feverish.

Billy had joined her husband and they sat together in the bleachers. Cockfighting was apparently not Gloria's dish—she didn't show. Billy looked surprisingly fresh considering the state I'd last seen her in, but she looked bored, too.

Ringo was trying to raise the bets. Though no one else felt the necessity of waving his money around, Ringo was doing it. His tone of voice was scornful; he was obviously feeling very superior—the natural sportsman.

One of his cocks had just been brought to the pit. "A thousand," he called. "A thousand on Ringo's Roundhead!"

There were no takers.

I was close enough to hear the conversation between Ringo and Billy. "Why don't you just stand up and tell them you're a big-time operator?" Billy asked him. "Go ahead and stand up! 'I'm Rand Ringo,' say. 'I'm the biggest operator in this section and in spots south and west. You want a bet on a sporting event, you peasants, you see Rand Ringo. Money talks and Rand Ringo's got it!' Go on. Stand up and tell them!"

"Shut up," Ringo said.

A few bets—for sums up to three hundred dollars, even money—were being made around the pit. Ringo scornfully spurned them.

"Bill your birds!" the referee said.

There was arrogance in Ringo's voice. He waved a handful of hundred-dollar bills. "Come on," he shouted. "Five to four. Five to four and a thousand on Ringo's Roundhead!" He paid casual, sidewise attention to the two cocks as they were billed. He watched them hackle and peck. Both birds looked fit and full of fight.

"Ready!"

It looked like a good fight and I wanted to see it. But Bigelow's Gray shake—the one he was so proud of—was on next and I had to heel him. On the way back to Bigelow's truck I stopped by the board to see if the match had been made. It had—with Ringo's Osceola.

Bigelow held the shake while I strapped his spurs and heeled him. He was a fighter. I could feel it in his quiet tenseness. I could sense it in the ferocity in his unblinking eyes as he stared at me as I worked. I could see it in the vicious, unrelenting way he stalked around as Bigelow walked him. The old man was babbling a little incoherently about his bird. I watched him carefully, then saw him stagger and almost fall. I wondered if he'd been hitting a bottle while I wasn't with him. Then I looked at his eyes, bright with fever, and I knew what I had to do. The old man was in no shape to handle another cock in the pit. I picked the Gray shake from the ground and laid him across my left arm. I faced the old man.

"I'm going to handle this bird for you," I said.

"I God, man—you're out of your mind. There ain't nobody going to—" He shook his head as if to clear it,

then went on: "I say there ain't nobody—" He
staggered again and caught himself on a fender of a
truck. He pressed a hand to a forehead and groaned.

"I'm going to handle this bird for you, O.D.," I
repeated, "and when this fight is over you're going to
a hospital."

He tried again to stand up to me, but his fight was
gone. He slumped against the fender. "Good luck to
you, son. Good luck—"

I turned to leave.

"And son—"

I stopped and looked at him.

"That cock means more to me than anything I
own."

I went to the pit. Ringo was there with his
Roundhead shake. He was going to handle him
himself, as Fee had said that he might. His eyes went
wide as he saw me, then hard, narrow, vicious. "All
right, Dolan," he said as I approached him. "I don't
know what you're trying to prove—but you're going a
little too far!" He turned from me. There had been no
time to explain and I was in no particular mood to
explain anyhow. I went to my side of the pit. Ringo
faced the bleachers and turned, slowly. "I've got five
thousand dollars that says this cock is a winner," he
said.

That was pretty big cockfight money in any league.
The crowd was silent, impressed.

"I'm offering five thousand dollars at five to four.
My five to anybody's four. Is there a sportsman in the
crowd?"

There were no takers. I watched Ringo look
defiantly at Billy. Billy looked away from him in
disgust.

"Five thousand at five to four. Come on! Come
on!"

Smaller bets were being made behind and around
me. Ringo's shake, because of its record and also

because of its slight weight advantage, was a two-to-one favorite. Ringo wasn't doing anybody any favors by offering five to four. He must have known this. Perhaps, I thought then, he really didn't want a bet.

"All right," he was saying now—and the arrogance in his voice was hard to take, "five to *three*. My five thousand against anybody's three thousand. An offer like this should separate the men from the boys!"

There were still no takers.

"Bill your birds!" the referee said.

He gave it another try. "Is there anyone in this crowd with guts enough to back the Gray for twenty-five hundred against my five thousand?"

They just wouldn't bet with him. They didn't like him. They wanted none of him except the use of his pit to fight their cocks. Ringo met me in the center of the pit and we billed the cocks and I saw to it that Ringo's Roundhead did most of the pecking. The Gray was quivering with rage when I returned to my score.

"Ready!"

I placed the Gray on the floor of the pit, holding him, waiting the five seconds for the call to pit. Ringo was slow moving to his score. It was his pit. He'd hired the referee and the referee could damned well wait.

"I won't make another offer. Is there a taker?"

I couldn't stand it any longer. "Sure. I'll take it," I said.

Ringo whirled. "How much of it?"

"All of it."

Somebody in the crowd laughed happily. Ringo's face was a mask of rage. "Do you want more?"

I shrugged. "Name it."

"Double it. Ten to five!"

I grinned. The five grand I was betting was the five grand Ringo had advanced me. Looking at it one way, I had nothing to lose. Easy come, easy go. "You're on," I said.

Behind me I heard Bigelow's quick and feverish voice. "I God, son, you give that slippery-assed son of a bitch a natural beating and I'll will you my house and farm in Tifton, Georgia. I'll do it just as sure as my name is O for Oscar, D for nothing, Bigelow!"

I turned and grinned at him, and when I did I saw Billy's face and it was no longer bored. Her eyes were bright with excitement as they met mine.

"Pit your cocks!"

The Gray raced straight for the Roundhead. The Roundhead, having won all its previous fights, was perhaps not as eager as the Gray. The Gray flew at him and the two cocks shot into the air, shuffling. The feathers—red and gray—flew. And when the cocks hit the dirt the Gray had a gaff in the Roundhead's left wing to the socket.

"Handle!"

Ringo and I were on the cocks before the word was out of the referee's mouth. Ringo's eyes were on mine, black and glittering, for the split second before he bent to remove the steel from his cock's wing. The Roundhead was not badly hurt, but he was a plenty mad cock now, and when we pitted again he met the Gray on the Gray's side of the pit, and it was he, the Roundhead, who broke this time on top, raking the Gray with the murderous steel. He failed to hang, however, and now they were on the ground matching beak to beak, and the crowd roared as they sparred, gaffs clicking, then shot again, shuffling. Again they hit the ground. This time the Roundhead had buried a gaff in the Gray's breast. The Gray was hurt. Not fatally— but badly enough.

I spent the twenty-second rest period before the next pitting dousing the Gray's head with water, stroking his back to ease him, slapping his head to madden him. There was no blood in his crop and though he was badly hurt I thought he might do.

"Pit!"

The Roundhead, flushed with success, again broke on top as the two cocks shot in the middle of the pit. They came down shuffling, angling against the wall of the pit. They rolled in the dirt and the call came to handle. The Roundhead had buried a gaff in the Gray's neck this time, just above the breastbone. Sweat was in my eyes and I slapped it away and bent to remove the gaff from the Gray's neck. As I worked I was barely conscious of Ringo's harsh whisper, "What about it now, Dolan? What about it now, bright boy?" And I walked back to my score, not looking at Bigelow, and I went to work. The Gray was in bad shape this time. I wasn't sure whether or not he was dying, but he was in very bad shape. I doused his head with water from the water can and I stroked his back. His crop was filling with blood and I sucked the blood away and spat it on the ground and I breathed into his open throat, trying to put some life into him.

"Pit!"

The Gray staggered, dead game, toward the Roundhead. The Roundhead met him and the Gray tried to shoot but couldn't make it and fell back onto the ground. The Roundhead had not been able to hang this time, but it didn't seem necessary. The Gray lay with his head in the bloody dirt and the Roundhead rutted around him, stopping to peck at his head occasionally, crowing, alert—the cock of the walk, having his moment before the crowd.

And the Gray lay there, his head torn and bloody, the upward eye still miraculously intact, and it seemed as if all the life left him was centered in that one eye. It was as fierce, as fighting mad, as ever before.

The match should have been moved to the drag pit. If it hadn't involved Ringo's prize cock, it would have been. The Gray kept it going by returning a feeble peck from time to time—and that's all it took to break the count.

Then suddenly, unbelievably, the Gray refused to let himself die. He got one leg under him, then the other—and he wobbled to his feet.

There was not a sound from the crowd.

The Roundhead was circling, stalking, waiting to move in for the kill.

From a corner of an eye I saw Billy Ringo move down to the railing of the pit. I shot a quick glance at her. Her eyes were shining, but not as before; they were hard now, and glittering, and there was something cruel about her mouth.

"Shoot, you Gray!" she shouted. "Shoot! Shoot! Shoot! little chicken!"

And then she screamed as the Gray shot valiantly to meet the Roundhead's shuffle. The two cocks went three feet into the air and seemed to hang there. And then they hit the ground in a welter of flying feathers and blood and one of the Gray's gaffs was buried in the Roundhead's head and the Roundhead was dead when Ringo picked him up.

The crowd poured into the pit and the first among them was O. D. Bigelow and the second among them was Billy Ringo. The old man cradled his Pure Law Gray to his chest and the tears poured down his leathery cheeks. Billy stood beside me and her breath came in quick gasps and savage triumph was naked on her face. Ringo walked across the pit and faced me. His lips were drawn in a smile, and his eyes spelled murder.

"All right, Dolan. It was a good fight. You'll have my check in the morning." He turned to his wife. "Come on, Billy," he said.

Billy looked at him. She didn't move.

Ringo blustered, "I said come on!"

Billy moved slightly, her shoulder brushing mine in an obvious gesture.

Ringo reached for her arm. She shrank from his touch.

I saw Ringo's eyes go to the group of men—dusty-eyed, sharp-cheeked, silent—beside and beyond him. He must have read the hatred in their faces.

"All right," he said.

Someone behind him laughed.

A hurt, bewildered, completely lost look came into his face—and I actually thought for a moment that he might burst into tears. As he left the pit a wave of sympathy for him swept me and I turned to Billy.

"Go with him," I said.

"If you tell me to," she said.

"Go with him," I repeated.

She left the pit and followed him.

Chapter Nine

I didn't see Ringo again that night. I left right after the cockfight with Bigelow—I'd made arrangements with an acquaintance of his to take care of his trucks and gamecocks—and I didn't go home until I'd put him under a doctor's care in the Cartersville hospital.

When I got home I showered, made myself a highball, put my .45 where I could reach it in a hurry, put a record on the phonograph, and sat down to do a little serious thinking on a purely personal matter, i.e., Dolan's future in Carter County.

From where I sat it didn't look good. Loy Bailey—after he'd talked with Adele—would almost certainly be gunning for me. My only real asset had been, before this afternoon, my standing with Ringo as his court favorite. But I had seen Ringo's eyes after that cockfight and I knew that he was a man who couldn't stand being beaten. I cursed myself for having gotten mixed up with the gnarly little Georgia cracker. Then I cursed myself for having been foolish enough to bet with Ringo. Ten thousand dollars was a lot of money—if I ever got it. But I felt fairly certain that I had, in the winning of it, killed the goose that laid the golden eggs. And that little scene with Billy in the cockpit after the fight had been cute, too. Real cute. Ringo, I decided, must love me, at this reading, like a long-lost son. I had one trump card, however, that made me of extreme incipient value to him: I knew what Adele and Loy Bailey were planning to do. Perhaps, with this information, I could buy off Ringo's hatred. Perhaps—

The telephone rang.

I turned the Capehart down and answered it. It was Sam Foster, Ringo's bolita man. He wanted to see me right away. I told him to come right out. He said he was on his way.

Sam's face was deeply troubled as I showed him into the front room. He didn't waste any words. He shoved a typewritten letter at me. I motioned him to a chair, took the letter, sat down and read it:

Sam Foster:
You will be out of Carter County, for good, by sundown the evening of August Six. This is the only warning you will have. Heed it or there will be a dead nigger before sunup August seven and that dead nigger will be you.

The Committee of Twelve.

August six was the next day.

"What will you do?" I asked Sam.

He stared at me. "What would you do, Mr. Dolan?"

"I'd get out of town. Out of the county. For good."

He was slow in answering me. "I somehow don't think you would. I somehow don't think you'd run from a thing like this, Mr. Dolan. You ain't running now, are you? And I hear you're in trouble with Mr. Ringo. Bad trouble. Word gets back to the quarters fast, Mr. Dolan. We know about things that happen around this county about as fast as they happen. You shouldn't never have gotten mixed up in that cockfight with Mr. Ringo. He can't stand to lose."

"Nobody's sent me any threatening letters."

"They got other ways of dealing with white folks."

"You think Ringo sent this letter to you?"

"He had it sent."

"Why?"

"Those things I was doing, or wasn't doing, that he sent you out to warn me about. I told you I wouldn't change my ways of doing things and I didn't. And two nights ago there was a meeting of the city commission. Those meetings are open to the public. It's law that they are, and the law don't say a thing about what color a man is as long as he's a taxpayer. The law says that any taxpayer has got a right to speak to the city commissioners at those meetings. I got up to ask the city commission to consider laying in some sidewalks in the quarters when they were preparing next year's budget. Folks out there has to walk in the roads. Two of our children been run down in the last year—run down on their way to school. One killed right off and the other one crippled. Those people there had never seen anything like that—a black man standing up to white men for the rights of his people. You'd have thought I had some bad sickness that they was all about to catch from me. I'd just gotten started talking when the mayor stood up and interrupted me. 'It's nine thirty-two,' he said, 'and these meetings are supposed to adjourn at nine-thirty sharp. The members of this commission have important engagements, I'm sure, and we can't hold them overtime. Write us a letter, Sam. We'll see it gets full consideration, won't we, boys?' He winked at them and they all grinned at him and they said, 'Sure,' and they all got up and hustled out of that room and left me standing there. My going to the meeting brought on that letter, there. But if it hadn't been that it would have been something else."

I didn't want to look at him just then. I stared at the floor. After a moment I raised my head and looked at him and said, "You're licked, Sam. Give up. I don't believe for a minute that these people would carry out their threat to you—but life won't be too pleasant for you if you stick around. To coin a cliché, you can't fight City Hall. In your case it applies. Literally."

"You don't think they'd try and harm me?"

"Not in this day and age."

He smiled sadly at me. "There's folks down here ain't found out yet what day and age it is, Mr. Dolan. Not many anymore, but some. People who've got to hate other people to keep from hating themselves. Let me fresh up your memory, Mr. Dolan. They killed Harry Moore and his wife at Mims on Christmas Eve of 1951." He spoke quietly. "They put a bomb under his house and they killed Harry Moore right out, and his wife died later in the hospital. They've bombed synagogues and colored real estate developments in Dade County within the year. Dade County's an hour and a little more in your automobile from here. They burned down the quarters in a race riot in Groveland a couple or so years ago. Groveland ain't but a little ways from here. There's plenty more things like that I could tell you. I ain't saying for sure they'd harm me. But they might."

I'd read about these things. The F.B.I. was still, if I remembered correctly, investigating the incidents out of their Miami office. It irritated me to have forgotten them. "I still think what you got was a crank letter. But if you think it might be serious, then that's all the more reason for you to leave."

"Maybe I got important reasons for staying, Mr. Dolan."

I didn't want to think about the kind of reasons I knew Sam was talking about. I'd done my thinking in foxholes and in hospitals and I knew what I wanted, and what I wanted had nothing to do with the sort of thing Sam was driving at.

"Goddamn it, Sam, what is it you want of me?"

"Talk to Mr. Ringo. About me."

"Try and get him to call off his dogs?"

"Yes, sir."

"You know how I stand with Ringo. You told me yourself."

"Maybe you got some way of getting back in good with him. Maybe you got something to trade."

I looked at him and his eyes told me nothing.

I glanced away. "I've got trouble enough of my own. Another man's troubles are of no concern to me, Sam."

"I somehow don't believe that, Mr. Dolan. I could sure be wrong. But most generally I'm right when it comes to figuring out a man. I told you once that your heart and your tongue don't meet. They still don't meet, Mr. Dolan. You're feeling one way on the inside and talking and doing another way on the outside. You been bad hurt somewhere along the line, Mr. Dolan, and you think you're trying to get even. And all you're doing is tearing yourself up inside."

"I know what I'm after. And I know what I'm doing. I didn't ask you out here to preach to me."

Sam stood. "You won't try and help me, Mr. Dolan?"

I wanted to get him out of there. I wanted to tell him to leave me alone. But he stood there in my doorway and he looked at me with those sad and knowing eyes and he was like some huge, shadowy conscience and I said to him, because I somehow couldn't help it, "I'll do what I can, Sam."

"I sort of figured you would, Mr. Dolan. Right from the start."

And then he was gone and I was left cursing myself for nineteen kinds of a chicken-hearted damned fool.

I tried to call Ringo the next morning and I was told that he had come in from his fishing lodge early that morning and had stayed there just long enough to pack and leave again. Nobody seemed to know where he had gone. I went to town. The day was another scorcher. Traffic crawled through the bouncing waves of heat and men were gathered in knots in the shade of doorways and under the rubber trees in the park. I parked my Ford in front of Boykin's Hardware and went inside for a couple of boxes of .45 ammo. A pasty-faced man—Boykin, I supposed—detached himself from the group of sweating men by the door and came to wait on me. I noticed, and ignored, one of Loy Bailey's pot-gutted deputies in the group. I told Boykin what I wanted.

"You ain't the only one," he said.

"So?"

"Next to hunting season, there ain't a thing in this world can beat an out-of-line nigger for stirring up the firearm and ammunition trade. Better than a special sale."

"What do you mean?"

"You mean you ain't heard about that Yankee-thinking nigger, Sam Foster?"

"No."

Boykin thought this was a scream. "Hey, boys," he called to the group by the door. "Here's a man ain't heard about Sam Foster!"

The men stared at me with dull, heat-glazed eyes. "Mallie Wilson there, from the sheriff's office, seen it and heard it. Seems this biggety nigger Sam Foster, from out in the quarters, here, come into the meeting of the city commissioners a couple of nights ago. It's a white folks meeting, naturally. Walked right into there like he thought he belonged there. Asked to speak and before the mayor could think of anything to say he went to talking. Went to telling the city commissioners they'd ought to vote money to lay in some sidewalks in the quarters! Ain't that a wheeze?"

A man in the group by the door—I recognized him now as Lon, one of the barbers—said, "Now what in hell you reckon a nigger would want with a sidewalk?"

I said nothing.

Boykin went on: "Mayor handled it real slick, though personally I would have thrown the fear of God into the black son of a bitch. Adjourned the meeting and everybody walked out of there and left the nigger talking."

"To himself," Lon added.

Mallie Wilson, the fat deputy, chewed the frazzled end of a cigar butt. His jowls were red and glistening with sweat. His shirt clung wetly to his chest and his thumbs were hooked beneath the heavily tooled Western belt that had slipped far down the slope of his swollen belly. "He stank," he said.

Boykin handed me my package.

A little bantam rooster sort of a man—I'd seen him hanging around the courthouse—said, "Us folks down here know how to treat the niggers—those of us old enough to remember how things was in the old days, that is. We never used to have much trouble with 'em, F.D.R.—him and his old lady—they're the ones ruined the niggers. And—"

Lon interrupted him. "You ain't just beating your gums, boy! All that talk about living wages and social equality and things such as that. And the F.E.P.C., that Roosevelt started and Truman kept trying to shove down our throats. Damn 'em all to hell. Why don't they leave us alone down here? We know what we're doing!"

A thin man with a long, disappointed face said, "Nigger man used to be worth a dollar a day. Nigger woman in your house, four, five dollars a week was good pay."

Boykin took over: "Less than that if she toted—took groceries home with her. All good hat-in-hand, yes-sir, yes-ma'am niggers, too. Field hand now wants, six, eight dollars a day. Woman wants fifteen, eighteen dollars a week to work in a house."

The bantam rooster said, "I blame it more on the schools. Way I look at it, no one in this country should be cheated out of a chance to learn to read and write and figure some. But four or five years' schooling is all in the world any nigger has got any use for. More than that don't do a thing but bring on trouble."

Mallie Wilson said, "Way I look at it, folks nowadays are just too easy on 'em. One thing, the state's full of snowbirds now—folks that've never been faced with the problem of living with the niggers. And all these young fellas, back from the war. That's another thing. Fighting alongside the niggers. And—"

Lon broke in again. "And these Yankee magazines, like *Time* and *Life*—calling nigger men mister and a nigger woman missus, and things like that. Making out like they was just as good as the whites."

The thin man said, "And religion today—that's another thing. Long as the people of this state were mostly good, God-fearing Southern Baptists and Methodists there wasn't no problem. You take a bunch of Episcopalians and Catholics and Lutherans and Jews and folks different like that, why they got no idea how to treat a nigger."

"You ain't just a'bird-turding, son," Boykin said. "You boys remember old Lem Whitlow, just for instance. Wasn't a more honest, God-fearing man in the section than old Lem Whitlow. Raised a family of twelve, paid cash money for everything he owned, was a deacon in the Baptist church for thirty-four years. Old Lem knew how to keep a nigger in his place. Remember that trip he took to Jacksonville on the Seaboard Airline away back yonder? He was standing on a platform between cars. Smart nigger porter come

along and give him some lip about how he wasn't
supposed to be there. Lem pulled his .44 and killed him
on the spot. Lem ran a big grove, one of the biggest in
the section. He never had any nigger trouble."

Two or three of the men laughed. "Old Lem,"
somebody said. "He was a great 'un, what I mean!"

"How about old Charley McDougald and his
boys?" Boykin went on. "You remember him, Mallie.
He wasn't no deacon, nor neither was his boys. But
they were good churchgoers. Old Charley and his boys
had a pack of Walker hounds that they'd trained to
chase nothing but niggers. There wasn't a thing in this
world old Charley and his boys would rather do than
to go on a nigger hunt. They loved that just the way
other men love to fox hunt. They'd take off through
the piney woods after their hounds. Hounds would
pick up nigger scent and off they'd go. Niggers all
knew about the hounds, knew they were vicious, and
when they heard 'em coming they'd take off like
Moody's goose. Times they'd get away. Mostly the
hounds would tree 'em—just like a dadburned coon!"

The thin man was showing brown teeth in a grin
that looked as if it hurt him. "Why, sure I remember
Charley, God rest him. And them boys of his, too. You
want a picnic, you should have seen one of them
niggers up a tree, his eyes rolling white, pleading with
Charley McDougald and those boys of his to call off
their hounds. And old Charley and his boys laughing
fit to kill."

"Old Charley." the bantam rooster said. "Tell me
the nigger mammies out in the quarters used to scare
their kids into being good by threatening them with old
Charley's hounds. Instead of 'the boogie man'll get you
if you don't do right,' it used to be, 'Mr. Charley's
hounds'll get you if you don't do right.' They tell me it
worked pretty well."

I was beginning to feel a little sick. I paid Boykin
for the shells. I walked toward the group in the

doorway. A couple of men moved to let me through. Mallie Wilson blocked the doorway. He stood there chewing that cigar stub and when I approached him he grinned a nasty little grin at me and he made no effort to move. I stopped in front of him. He still didn't move. I reached forward in a sweeping motion and knocked the cigar butt from his mouth to the floor. I wiped my hand on my trouser leg and said, "When a cigar is done, throw it away. Move, you barrel-assed bastard!"

His mouth gaped like a dying catfish's and he stood there staring at me for a split second and then he moved aside.

I stood on the sidewalk, slatted sweat from my forehead, then crossed the street and walked slowly through the park. Several groups of men stood in the shade of the rubber tree. Someone in each group was talking. I heard two references to "that black son of a bitch." I hurried on to the drinking fountain. I stopped there for a drink of cool water. Two grizzled old men sat on the bench beside it. One of them was saying, in a thin, querulous, old man's voice, "... can say what you want to, no man's ever done as much for this city and this county as Rand Ringo ..."

I went to my Ford and drove angrily home.

Chapter Ten

I tried calling Ringo a half-dozen times during the afternoon, and just after dark I made the trip out to his house on the chance that he might be there and was simply trying to avoid me. I'd promised Sam Foster I'd do what I could to help him and I had no intention of reneging on my promise. Besides that Ringo had promised me my check for ten thousand that morning and I'd seen nothing of it. He had me off-balance again. He had me guessing. I wanted to know how I stood with him. If I was all through in Carter County I wanted to know about it. I wanted to be on my way.

I didn't like standing around with my bare face hanging out.

I made my way to the front door of that monstrous monument to vulgar wealth and bad taste and I rang the doorbell. Ben answered it. The hall led straight from the front door to Ringo's office and I thought I saw a shadow shift at the end of the hall.

"Mr. Ringo in, Ben?"

Ben's ryes rolled. He seemed frightened. "I ain't seen Mr. Ringo since early this morning, Mr. Dolan, sir."

I said quietly, "Ben, you're lying to me."

"No sir, I wouldn't lie none to you, Mr. Dolan!" I got the impression there was something he'd like, but was afraid, to tell me.

"I've got to see him, Ben. It's important."

"Like I said, he ain't here, Mr. Dolan."

I thought of brushing the old man aside and having a look for myself but I decided against it. "All right, Ben," I said. "Will you ask Mr. Ringo to call me when you see him? Tell him it's very important."

"Yes, sir, Mr. Dolan."

I turned and left him. Halfway between the house and my Ford was the banyan tree where I'd once seen Gloria Ringo. I remembered my morbid thoughts then. I looked at the great tree again. Moonlight burnished its leaves but darkness squatted in the recesses formed by its twisting trunks and its downward-groping arms, and there was an evil beauty about its rapacious growth that made me shudder again. I was almost past it when my name was spoken softly.

"Brad—"

I wheeled as Gloria stepped from under the banyan into the moonlight.

"I—I saw your car."

She was lovely and I wanted her in my arms, but she was trouble—and I had trouble enough. "Yes?" I said.

"Couldn't we talk? Couldn't we go somewhere and finish talking about some of the things we started talking about by the springhouse?"

"Why?"

Her great eyes were deeply troubled. "Why are you hurting me?"

I was weakening. I wanted to touch her. I wanted to taste her lips again. I wanted to feel the beat of her heart against mine. "I'm not trying to hurt you, Gloria. It's just that we started something we can never finish," I said. "There's no use dragging it out."

"Brad—" And then she was in my arms, and her lips were soft and sweet against my own. Then she took my hand firmly, and led me across the shimmering lawn to the boathouse by the river. The speedboat coughed once, then purred, as I cast off the lines. And then it roared as Gloria gunned it, and the wake behind us roiled and danced in the moonlight as we sped down the river.

Twenty minutes later Gloria throttled down and nosed the boat gently toward the shoreline and I made it fast to the remains of a dock. A bluff loomed above us and I recognized it as the same one I'd seen before— her grandfather's old homeplace—and we climbed the hill and sat on the same ruined beam we'd sat on before.

I took her hand. It was cold. She turned to me, and I saw that she was deeply disturbed.

"Brad," she said, "what's the matter with my father?"

I said slowly, "What do you mean?"

"He's—he's been acting so strangely lately. I don't know exactly how to explain it, really. But he's changed so much. He was always so kind, so considerate.... Or maybe I've just grown up, that's all. Maybe he's always been the same and I've just never noticed it. The way he treats Billy, for instance—the way he goads Billy into rebellion and then seems so startled, so hurt, when she turns on him. And the way he treats me—like a child. He doesn't seem to realize that I'm a grown woman now. I can ride his horses, drive his cars or his boat, swim in his pool—anything. But I've nothing of my own. Not even my own identity! I seem to be gradually changing from Gloria Ringo to Rand Ringo's daughter.

"I'm through school. I've come home to live. I'd like to take some active part in his cattle or his citrus business. I'd like to be useful, active. He won't even allow Billy or me in his kitchen. He plans everything himself—even the menus. He just smiles condescendingly and says, 'Run along and play, kitten,' when I try and ask him something about his business. And the dinners we have, when other people are there. You've seen how he is. He doesn't seem happy unless he is completely dominating the conversation. It's as if he were holding the conversational hoop and making people jump through it.

"I remember when I first went to Sunday school and was taught about God. I suppose everyone forms his own mind picture of God. For a long time I thought of him as a jolly, white-bearded, Santa Claus type who loved everyone, even sinners, but loved them with a sweet and undemanding love. And then I liked him a lot. But now when I think of God all I can see is my father, dominating everyone's lives, bending people to his own will, enfolding them, smothering them. And I don't like God very much anymore. I love my father because somehow I'm sorry for him. But I don't like him, because I'm afraid of him!"

She was shivering. I held her close to me.

"I don't know what to think. I'm not the only one who's afraid. Other people are, too. I've seen it! I've watched people who've come to see him on business. And Billy, and even Ben and all the help. They're all afraid of him, Brad, everyone but you. Why is it? Is there something evil about him that everyone can see but no one will talk about? I've got to know. Is there, Brad?"

"Your father's a powerful man, Gloria. People always fear power."

"Why is he so powerful? What sort of a hold does he have on this county? I told you before I'd heard ugly rumors. I told you I didn't believe them. I didn't, then. But now I don't know. I want to be loyal to him. He's all I've got. But I feel as if I've just come awake—and I feel it's you who's awakened me. I was sleepwalking, Brad, and you've shaken me awake. I can't refuse to see things or think about them any longer."

You think twice, or maybe three times, before you speak the words that complete a person's disillusionment in someone he or she has loved. And any truthful explanation I might give Gloria of Ringo's hold over the county would cut my own throat as well. Ringo and I were passengers on the same gravy train. I wasn't exactly a junior partner but I was knee-deep in the same slime and had five thousand dirty bucks, or thereabouts, in the bank to prove it. And I somehow didn't want Gloria to know that.

I stroked her hand. "Nerves," I said. "You got 'em bad. You're dreaming it up, honey. Ringo's not a simple guy—none of us is. It's all going to come out in the wash. I personally guarantee it."

She stared at me. "Is it that simple?"

"It's that simple. And I'm going to change the subject. Look, you're a bug on inland Florida. How's that for a concentrated slice of inland Florida scenery?" The river coiled black and silver below us, and the leaves of the wild orange trees gleamed in the moonlight.

She brightened. "Lovely, isn't it?"

"Delightful," I said.

"You're pulling my leg."

"I wouldn't think of it."

"You are, and I know it. But I don't care—I love this kind of country. I love everything about it."

"Including the rattlesnakes and the sandspurs and the palmetto scrub?"

"You're like all the rest—the outsiders, the people who don't know, who think Florida is just a ring of golden beaches, and that inside the ring there isn't much of anything. A few oranges, maybe. And of course Silver Springs where Ross Allen milks the snakes and Dick Pope's Beautiful Cypress Gardens where beautiful girls do beautiful tricks on water skis."

"You sound bitter."

"I'm not bitter. It's just that here, in Central Florida, we all *do* something. There's all this important industry—cattle, citrus, phosphate, and so on—and people don't even *know* about it. Or if they do they don't care. I got it all the time at school. It was always, 'How far are you from Hobe Sound?' or, 'Do you know so and so who built this fantastically beautiful and expensive home in Naples?' and when I would try and explain Central Florida to them they would start feeling sorry for me."

As long as we kicked things like this around she wouldn't get morbid about Ringo. "They tell me Florida and Southern California are among the last natural habitats of the old-fashioned remittance man. That so?"

"All on the beaches. Remittance men, boat bums, beachcombers in sandals and Brooks Brothers' walking shorts."

"Sweating out their inheritance?"

She nodded. "If you've already got it, or if you've done well and you've retired, you build a forty- or a fifty-thousand dollar home, made mostly of glass, on a fill or behind a sand dune. And then you buy a cabin cruiser and you fish the Gulf Stream if you've built from Delray south to Miami, or you fish Boca Grande Pass through the Ten Thousand Islands to Shark River if you've built your house from Sarasota south to Naples."

"I know the rest of it," I said. "You think the natives all have hookworm and you think the state politics are quaint and you think the Brahman steers are interesting critters—that hump, and all, and you bake out last night's drinks on the hot sands, and after a few years you're a real Florida cracker; with sand in your shoes—but that doesn't keep you away from New England from May to October—"

"Love that sunshine!"

"But what's happened to the common man? There must be some poor folks. In from the outside, I mean. Yankees, and that kind of trash."

"You find them in trailer camps. Or small apartments. In St. Petersburg or Vero Beach or Bradenton or towns like that, where the sun is almost always warm on the benches, and where there are more shuffleboard courts and undertakers and retired farmers and small businessmen from Ohio and Iowa than in any other towns in the world."

I stroked her hand. "Get off the soapbox, honey."

She smiled at me. "I feel real soapboxy tonight, darling. But I'd rather be soapboxy about you and me. I asked you a question back at the house—just for instance. I asked you why you're hurting me." Her voice became very serious. "This week-end you hurt me, too. On the dock. You wouldn't stay, you wouldn't talk. You've avoided me since the day we were first here. Tonight, at first, you didn't want to come with me. You said something horrible about having started something we couldn't finish. I don't believe that. Why are you hurting me?"

"I haven't meant to," I said lamely.

"You know what? I think you've been hurt yourself. Badly. And you're all defense mechanism now. You've pulled back behind a protective wall of scar tissue and bitterness and you're afraid to come out

for fear you'll be hurt again. And that's why—
unconsciously, perhaps—you're hurting me. Bitterness
is selfishness, Brad, you know—self-pampering. If I
hadn't seen you and held you closely when you came
out from behind those defenses I wouldn't mind. But
that's what hurts—to have seen you as you really are.
The afternoon we spent here and at the pool is very
special and very beautiful to me, Brad. Or am I being
a fool to think that it was? What's hurt you, Brad? You
were married once—was that it? Tell me about your
being married, Brad."

"It was just a phase. A growing-up phase."

"Were you happy? For a while?"

"I suppose so. I don't know. Maybe I just thought
I was. She was very beautiful. Maybe I just liked being
seen with her. Perhaps the happiness I thought I was
having with her was all tied up with being five or six
years younger than I am now and living and working
in New York for the first time, and being a part of the
quickness and the excitement and the hopefulness of it
all. There was always plenty of money because my wife
was making plenty. There were all the good shows and
week-ends on the Sound in the summer, or at
Smuggler's Notch when the snow was right for skiing.
Good music at Carnegie Hall or in the little joints
along Fifty-Second Street. That's the way it was. I
suppose I was happy. I didn't have time to figure it
out."

"What stopped your happiness?"

"I made an interesting discovery. I discovered that
my wife was a tramp."

"But you can't forget her. You can't, can you? The
memory of her is there with you, inside you, and you'll
never belong to anyone else until you can forget her,
or until you're sure you're no longer in love with her.
Oh, Brad—Brad, darling—there's something I've got
to tell you. There's something you must know. I—"

"Yes?"

Her lips worked as she made an effort to speak.

"It must be pretty important."

She looked deeply at me for a moment. Then she turned her head and stared out over the river. "No," she said. "I'm sorry. It's—it's nothing. I'm sorry I brought it up."

She was shivering again. I cupped her face in my hands and I looked at her, and her slightly parted lips were trembling and her eyes were crying out to me and I kissed her, gently. "Brad, Brad, Brad, darling," she moaned softly as we stretched full-length in the grass. "I'll make you forget her. I'll make you love me. I will! I will! Now, Brad! Now, darling. Now!"

And I took her then, gently. I took her with pride and with humility. Our loving was right and natural, and our joy in it was the ecstasy of healthy adult animals in need of each other.

It was hours later when I headed the boat home. Her head was nestled in the hollow of my shoulder and I could smell the sweet freshness of her hair, made sweeter, fresher, by the scent of the rich grass, and I wondered what more any man could want than such a woman beside him, forever. And I cursed myself for thinking these thoughts because I knew that what Gloria had said about Dusty was true. I could never completely belong to any other woman than Dusty until I had forgotten her, or until I had been shocked out of her.

I took Gloria to her door. The house was dark. She turned to me. "Thank you, my darling," she whispered. I hushed her with a kiss and her finger tips trailed softly along my cheek as I turned and left her.

I drove slowly home, thinking, thinking hard. When I got home I was still deep in thought. I poured myself a stiff drink and took the drink into my bathroom to shower. Billy Ringo was there—on the floor. Her dress was torn and twisted around her thighs. She was no longer beautiful, because her throat had been cut, and my straight razor lay in a pool of blood beside her and she was very dead.

Chapter Eleven

I knew then—once and for all—that I'd overstayed my welcome in Carter County. I closed the bathroom door to shut out the sight of Billy lying there in her own blood, but I knew when I did it that it was a foolish, useless act. I'd seen friends of mine dead in their own blood before and I could never forget the sight of them and I knew I'd wake up nights for the rest of my life seeing Billy Ringo as she was lying there now on my bathroom floor.

I sat down and tried to figure it out, and my mind whirled and fluttered like a rag in a gale. The only thing I knew for sure was that Billy Ringo hadn't done this thing to herself. Her dress was torn and twisted; she'd struggled and she'd fought for her life. And even if she hadn't, I'd have known: when you're tired of living you don't cut your throat with a straight razor— you pick an easier way.

I knocked off the bourbon in a gulp and when I poured another stiff hooker from the bottle I noticed that my hand was shaking. I went into my bedroom to dress and while I was dressing I tried to chart a course. The first step, naturally, would be to call the law. And the law was Loy Bailey and company, and I almost felt like laughing as I thought of the chance I'd stand with them. Should I beat it? Get in my Ford and head for parts unknown? My chances of getting clear would be slim. And running out now would be an admission of guilt. I'd have to stay and fight this thing. And from where I sat, tilting at windmills made more sense. I didn't know what to do. Then I heard the sound of a car slithering to a stop, the slam of a car door, then the clomp of several pairs of heavy feet on the front porch, and a series of loud knocks, and I realized, with some relief, that the decision was no longer mine.

I went to the door and opened it on Loy Bailey and two of his deputies. One of the deputies was the one who'd blocked my exit at Boykin's Hardware. He was chewing on the stub of another cigar and grinning his nasty little grin at me, and his eyes were daring me to do something about that cigar butt.

"I've been expecting you, boys," I said.

Bailey narrowed his pig eyes at me. "Why?"

"You answer that one, Loy," I said.

"I'll ask the questions, bum. You'll answer them. Billy Ringo's turned up missing. Ringo's out of town. The people out at Ringo's house have been told to keep tabs on her when the boss is away. The nigger butler out there called me. And I'm looking for her."

"So why come here?"

"Don't hand me that crap."

I forced a grin. "I think I know now who trampled my azaleas. A peeping Tom, huh, Loy?"

Bailey fought to control himself. "So I saw you two in the sack. I needed something on you and I got it. How do you think Ringo's going to like it when he knows you've been sleeping with his wife? I've been saving that one, bum, until I really needed it."

"How's Adele, Loy? You two been having any long talks?"

Bailey's face paled. "Is Billy here, Dolan?"

"She's here, all right."

"Where?"

"In the bathroom."

"Keep an eye on him," Bailey told his deputies. He started for the bathroom.

"You wouldn't walk in on a lady while she's in the bathroom, would you?" I said.

I watched to see if he'd knock. He did, but I couldn't tell whether he was doing it for my benefit or not. He waited a minute, then knocked again. He opened the door.

"Christ!"

His ugly face was bluish-green as he faced us. "See if he's clean," he shouted to his deputies, "then shackle him! The son of a bitch has cut her throat!"

The deputies relieved me of my pocket knife and my wallet, then handcuffed me. Loy called the coroner, then crossed the room to me. His color had returned.

"You've had it, bum," he said. "You're all through." His shoulders twitched and he telegraphed the roundhouse right he threw at my chin, but my reflexes had been slowed by the course of events and the room seemed to explode in flashes of light before it went black. If I hit the floor hard I didn't know it because I was sound asleep.

I woke up in darkness, too, but I knew where I was because I'd been there before. The same slimy floor, the same stinking mattress. From somewhere down the cell block I could hear the frightened moans of some poor devil fighting a bad drunk. Two or three cells down from me and across the passageway a Negro was coaxing minor chords from a guitar and singing a song in a blue and troubled key.

"Sometimes I feel like a motherless child,
Sometimes I feel like a motherless child,
Sometimes I feel like a motherless child,
A long ways from home, a long ways from home,
O—Lawdy, a long ways from home."

My head throbbed and my jaw was stiff and sore. I moved it, tentatively, and decided that it had at least not been broken. I stood up, unsteadily, and groped for a cigarette—at least they'd unshackled me—found one, lighted it, and took a deep drag. I felt a little better. The chords floated from the guitar across the passageway and hung throbbing in the stale air:

"Sometimes I feel like I never been borned,
Sometimes I feel like I never been borned,
Sometimes I feel like I never been borned,
I know my time ain't long, I know my time ain't
long,
O—Lawdy, I know my time ain't long."

Appropriate music, I thought. Book by Rand Ringo, music by unknown culprit, direction by Loy Bailey, starring that dynamic personality, Brad Dolan.

I shook my head to clear it. The guitar and the song went on:

"Sometimes I feel like a feather in the air,
Sometimes I feel like a feather in the air,
Sometimes I feel like a feather in the air,
A long ways from home, a long ways from home,
O—Lawdy, a long ways from home."

You've pegged it, brother, I thought. *You've sung it right and true!* The door to the cell block opened. The guitar chords throbbed away into nothingness as the old jailer clumped down the corridor to my cell.

"Dolan?" He peered in.

"The same," I said.

"I'm a suck-egg mule if I ever did see a man in and out of a jailhouse like you." His voice went querulous. "You'd think I didn't have nothing more to do than let you in and out of this cell."

"My apologies," I said.

His voice brightened. "One good thing, though, they tell me with what you've gone and done now, you'll be cooling your ass in here till God-comes-Friday. Or at least until you're transferred to the state prison at Raiford."

"Every cloud has got a silver lining, Pop," I said.

"And all that glisters ain't gold, as the old feller says. Come on. The sheriff wants to talk with you."

"Good," I said. "They tell me conversation is a lost art. The sheriff is a charming man. I'm sure we'll find we have lots of things in common to talk about."

He unlocked the cell door and swung it open. He kept one hand on the gun on his hip and motioned me toward the open cell-block door and followed me through it into the room beyond it. Loy Bailey and the two deputies who had been with him earlier were sitting there drinking coffee and waiting for me. A pot of coffee was being kept hot on an electric grill on a desk. The smell of that coffee was out of this world and I would have given plenty for a cup of it but I wouldn't ask Bailey for it.

"I want a lawyer," I said. "I want to call Miami and get a lawyer up here."

Bailey smirked. "You hear that, boys?" he said to his deputies. "He wants a lawyer. He has some kind of a lover's spat with another man's wife and he cuts her throat from ear to ear and he thinks a lawyer will do him some good!" He turned to me. "All right, bright boy. The law says you're entitled to legal defense. When the time comes I'll get you a lawyer. But the time ain't come!" He stood. "Come on," he said to me. "Me and my associates here have got a couple of questions we'd like answered."

He crossed the room, opened a side door, and motioned me into the room beyond it. It was a small, low-ceilinged, bare room with peeling, discolored paper on its walls. A stained shade was drawn the length of the only window. There was one chair in the room. In front of the chair was a flood lamp. Across the room was a desk. On the desk were half a dozen eighteen- or twenty-inch pieces of ordinary garden hose and a disconnected recording machine. On one wall was a framed picture of George Washington—the reproduction that used to be standard equipment in

school rooms when I was a kid. Nice, I thought. A
well-appointed room. A great place to relax from the
trials and tribulations of a busy, heartless world.

"Plug in the flood lamp, Mallie," Loy said.

Mallie, the fat deputy, did as he was told. Loy
turned out the overhead light.

"Great little place you have here," I said.
"Somebody with good taste spent a great deal of time
and thought doing this room. And it's so personal. I
love a room that reflects the personality of its
decorator, don't you, Sheriff?"

"Sit down, bum!"

"There's only one chair. I wouldn't think of—"

"Sit down!"

There didn't seem to be much else to do. I sat in
that chair and the light from that flood lamp bit into
my eyes.

"That's better," Loy said. He sounded almost
reasonable now. "You had any breakfast? Maybe
you'd like a cup of coffee."

I nodded.

"Mallie!"

Mallie left the room and returned with a cup of
steaming coffee. He handed it to Loy.

"We can't let a man go without coffee in the
morning, can we, boys?" He said, "That wouldn't be
nice, would it, boys?"

He threw the coffee in my face. It was hot enough
to make me stifle a scream and for a split second the
room was whirling black with red around the edges
and I started out of that chair, swinging blindly, but
the bruising sting of a rubber hose across the side of
my face and neck knocked me back into the chair. I
clawed at my eyes and shook my head, and then Loy
Bailey's grinning face swam back into focus.

"That might give you some kind of an idea who's
boss farmer around here, bright boy. Why'd you kill
her?"

"I want a lawyer."

"Why'd you kill her?"

"You know I didn't kill her, Bailey."

This time the rubber hose caught me across my chin and mouth and I tasted the saltiness of my blood and felt the swelling numbness of my lips.

"Why'd you kill her?"

I said nothing.

"Why, goddamn it?"

I shook my head to clear it and said nothing.

"Hold off a minute, boss," Mallie said. He lighted the stub of his cigar, puffed it a couple of times, then took it from between yellowed teeth and held it close to my bare arm.

"Ask him again, boss."

"I'm asking you why you killed her, Dolan."

I said nothing.

"This smart son of a bitch don't like ceegar butts, boss," Mallie said. "'When a ceegar is done,' he says, 'why, throw it away.' I'm aiming to show this smart son of a bitch that a good ceegar butt can come in handy."

He ground the lighted butt into my forearm.

I smelled the sickening smell of burning flesh and the pain came in red and yellow and purple waves and my stomach twisted and knotted and I vomited.

"Jeeesus, chief," the other deputy said. "We got to put up with *that*? Him puking all over the place?"

My head was reeling. I fought for consciousness.

"All right, bum," Bailey said. "We'll put it this way. You didn't do it, you say. That right?"

I nodded.

"You just went home and found her there. Right?"

"That's right."

"All right. Where were you last night? Where were you, bright boy?"

"Out. Just out, that's all."

"With who?"

I wouldn't get Gloria mixed up in this thing—not if I could help it.

"With nobody. I was driving. I couldn't sleep and I wanted fresh air and I was just driving. It's a habit of mine. It makes me sleepy."

Bailey laughed hoarsely. "Hear that, boys? This bum here is a real sensitive type bum. Likes to drive around at night alone. Likes to look at the stars and feel the breeze in his face. A mighty peculiar type bum, ain't he, boys?"

"I want a lawyer," I said.

"Shut up," Bailey said, and he slapped me across the face. "You remember the first time we picked you up? The time you started that brawl out at Joe's place? We fingerprinted you that night over at my office at the courthouse. You were passed out drunk on the bench in my office but we got your prints. The fresh prints on that straight razor beside Billy Ringo—the *only* prints on that razor—are yours, Dolan."

"So what?" I said.

"Goddamn you!" Bailey screamed. "A man can take just so much!" He swung on me with his rubber hose. I felt the first blow across my face to the marrow of my bones; the second was a dull, indifferent, impersonal sort of a pain, and the third one didn't hurt at all. I felt myself slumping, then slipping from the chair to the floor, and then my only sensation was a vast, bruised tiredness. Sleep, I remember thinking—if I could just get some sleep—

But how could a man sleep? The night before had been a tough one, and the night before that, too, and all the nights reaching back into a dark and noisome tunnel for as far as a man could see or remember. The platoon had dug in around that reservoir on 'Canal—or was it just outside that ruined village with the unpronounceable name on Korea—two, three, ten nights before. And the Japs, Gooks, whichever they were—if I could hear them shout "To hell with Yanks" I could tell whether they were Japs or Gooks and then I would remember where I was, because if they were Japs they'd screw up their *l*'s and then I would know— had come screaming down that wooded slope three, seven nights in a row. And we'd caught them in our field of fire the first few nights and the bodies had piled high, but last night and the night before the firing had become point-blank, and then it was bayonets and clubbed M-1's, and then, miraculously, they had stopped coming.

I could hear them chattering now, like monkeys, a hundred yards up the slope, behind a rocky abutment, and I listened to hear the way they said their *l*'s but I couldn't hear them so I couldn't tell. Perhaps they'd blow a bugle. Then I would know. If I had water I could think more clearly. There were fourteen of us left in the platoon—or had that been yesterday morning? Was it eight now? Eight men with gravelly eyes, mud-caked lips, and fear-loose bowels.

The chattering behind the abutment was growing louder and louder and I pressed into the earth waiting for the first *whoosh* of the incoming mortar round that would start the softening up process for the next attack. And all I wanted was water.

I opened a swollen eye and stared at the pocked and splintery floor. My body ached and throbbed from head to toe. My throat felt choked with cotton and my mouth was brassy with the taste of old blood. My head was pillowed on one arm and I didn't have the strength to move.

I heard, as if from far away, the voice of the fat deputy, Mallie. "What now, boss?"

"When he comes out of it take him back to his cell. Give him a chance to think it over. Then we'll bring him back. Next time I think he'll talk plenty."

"You know what I been thinking, Loy?" Mallie said, "I been thinking that when the State tries this guy for murder there's bound to be some things brought out that ain't favorable to us. After all, this guy knows the family secrets—or most of them. I mean the way this county is run, and all. Seems to me like all that is bound to be brought out when bright boy, here, goes on the stand."

"You're a dumb bastard, ain't you, Mallie?"

"Now wait a minute, Loy. What do you—"

"This bum ain't never going to stand trial, Mallie."

"No?"

"This bum will be shot down trying to escape. Only thing I'm waiting for is his confession. And after one more session in here I think I'll get it. I ain't had breakfast, boys, and I can't remember when I've been hungrier. Throw a basin of water on this son of a bitch and get him back to his cell. I might have time to work him over again today and I might not. It's going to be a busy day. And I'm going out to Ringo's fishing lodge tonight. That's between us. If anybody asks you, you won't know where I'm at. There's pretty apt to be some exciting things going on around town tonight— things a good sheriff has got no right to see, and I don't aim to be around to see them."

Chapter Twelve

They left me alone the rest of the day. The day floated by on wings of fever and throbbing pain and dreams. I lay sweating on that filthy mattress and I dreamed my dreams. One, I remember, was of Ringo, and Ringo's face was huge and evil and his great, luminous eyes shone above a backdrop painted to represent the town of Cartersville. And his huge hands, above this backdrop, were controlling strings, and dangling from the strings were puppets.

I looked closely at the puppets and I saw, with horror, myself; myself moving stiffly, mechanically, across the stage, toward another puppet that was Gloria Ringo. And I had almost reached her outstretched arms when Ringo laughed, an evil laugh, and Billy Ringo came onstage, between us, swaying drunkenly, blood pouring from her slit throat. And then Billy was laughing at me and Loy Bailey and his deputies came on stage, then Sam Foster, Ben, Adele, Virgie Lupfers, Al Hastings, Pop the jailer, Demetrios, the desk clerk at Cartersville's Home Away From Home, Al the cabby, Joe Fanchon, the fat man who couldn't trap a fly, the barbers, Adele's huge Negro masseur, the man who had stood up for a Nash Rambler, Boykin the hardware man—the entire cast— were brought on-stage by Ringo the puppeteer, and they were all pointing at me—all but Gloria, Billy, and Sam Foster—and chanting, "You killed her, you killed her!" And Ringo spun his puppets in a mad dance around me, and the chanting grew faster and faster and Ringo's laughter was like thunder in the sky, and-

"Hot almighty, boy!" I heard the old jailer say. "You been squealing like a Georgia mule. You think I got nothing better to do of a hot August afternoon than to set around listening to you squeal in your sleep? Gets on a man's nerves. Here. Drink this."

He handed me a tin dipper full of ice water. I sat up shakily. My face hurt like hell. I drained the dipper and felt a little better. Then I took the ice that was left in the dipper, wrapped it in my handkerchief, and smoothed it against my swollen lips and face.

"That's better. Thanks, pop."

"They were pretty rough on you, hey, boy?"

"I can take anything they can dish out."

"Pretty tough fella, huh?"

"When you're right and they're wrong, they can't hurt you. They can muss you up but they can't hurt you, inside."

"You mean to set there and tell me you didn't kill that girl?"

"That's what I'm saying."

He stared at me for a moment. "Who you reckon killed her, son?"

"I wouldn't know. Somebody who wanted Billy Ringo out of the way, and me, too, and figured that was a good way of doing it. Two birds with one stone. Very slick. I don't know who wanted Billy dead. Loy Bailey wants me out of the way. And a woman called Adele. And maybe even Ringo."

The old man was frightened. He lowered his voice and fastened his rheumy old eyes on mine. "They're a bad lot," he half-whispered. "Bad! Treat me like a goddamn old hound dog around here, working my ass off day and night, or I wouldn't say a word. I've seen some things go on around this jailhouse that'd make the hair stand up on a bullfrog! I've heard 'em screaming in that room they had you in today. I've heard 'em screaming and I've seen 'em carted out of there in a basket, too. What'd they use on you today?"

"Hoses. And a lighted cigar butt."

"Bailey's got worse than that. Whips. Lighted matches under your nails. Ice picks. Turpentine where it hurts the worst. Castor oil. Bailey knows his business. I've seen him break a nigger's jaw without leaving a mark on him. He laid a towel across his jaw and—"

I interrupted him. "Spare me the details, pop. I've got troubles enough."

"And Ringo. He's the worst of the lot. I been around here a long time, boy, and I could tell you a thing or two about Ringo, if I was of a mind to. I've tried to tell these things before, but there ain't anybody around town will pay me any mind. Say I'm a windy old fart with a grudge to nurse. That's the way everybody is around this town and this county. Ringo, as far as they're concerned, can't do no wrong.

Donates to the churches. Gives ground for a new schoolhouse. Buys the hospital an X-ray machine. Throws a big barbecue for a thousand people three times a year. Calls everyone by his first name. They all claim to think he's the greatest man ever to come down the big road. But you know what? They really don't like him. They hate him. But they're afraid of him. The bastards are scared to death!"

"I've seen it happen before."

"They'll tell you his old daddy starved to death because he was proud. That might be partways true. But I knew old Thad Ringo well. Many's the time we've spent the night setting around a smudge fire passing a jug of corn back and forth and listening to his hounds and mine bay up a warm trail. I'll tell you what killed Thad Ringo. It was heartbreak. His heart broke when he seen the way his only boy was going. And maybe you've heard how Ringo's first wife died. A hunting accident, they called it. Her and Ringo was in a duck blind, alone. She shot herself—'accidentally.' Blew the side of her head off. Quite a little to-do about that then—but people forget. Maybe it was an accident—but Ringo's wife had hunted all her life. She could knock down more ducks out of a flight than most men. She was a handsome Yankee woman, and rich—real rich. And there was some talk around town before she died that she'd caught Ringo laying up with a good-looking high yaller and was fixing to leave him."

"You hate him plenty, huh, pop?"

"Let me tell you how Ringo got started in the cattle business. There was an old man named Snap Bence owned fifty thousand acres of rangeland along the river—out where Ringo's house is at now. Snap had land, but no money. After Ringo's wife died Ringo had money—plenty of it. He made old Snap a proposition and they threw in together, became partners, and started developing and stocking Snap's land with

Ringo's money. One day the two of them were 'way off to the far corner of that land on horses. Ringo came back that evening with Snap across his saddle—dead. Said Snap's horse had shied at a rattlesnake and thrown Snap and he'd landed headfirst on a slash pine stump and fractured his skull. His head was caved in, all right; there was even rosin matted in his hair. Could of been a slash pine stump. But a pine knot makes a mighty fine weapon! Snap had no family. Ringo had sucked up to him so's the old man had come to look on him as a son. Who do you think got that fifty thousand acres? Ringo!"

"That's all hearsay, pop. You're second guessing."

"You're damned tootin' it's hearsay. But where there's smoke there's fire!"

"What have you got against him personally, pop?"

The old man's mouth worked. "He's kin to me, see," he blurted out. "Thad Ringo was my brother, and Rand's my nephew. 'We got to look after our own, George,' the bastard told me after I lost my farm in '36. 'Blood is thicker than water,' he said, 'though he'd never thought of it when I needed the money to save my farm. So he had me made jailer here. I got to live down here watching misery day in and day out and run my ass ragged for Loy Bailey and his goddamn deputies. For a while I asked Rand for something better. 'George,' he'd say, and smile. 'I'd like to do something better for you—and maybe I will. But we've got to remember your weakness—'"

The old man's eyes filled with futile tears. "All right," he told me. "I'll admit I got a yen for good corn whisky. I'll admit I've put away many a gallon in my life. I'll admit I never did amount to a hill of cow peas all my life. But the son of a bitch could have made me something more than a turnkey for his own private goddamn pesthouse!"

I stood and grasped the old man's shoulder. "Pop," I said quietly, "get me a lawyer."

His eyes dulled and his mouth went slack. "I been talking too much. Too much." He wouldn't look at me. "Old man's talk."

"Get me a lawyer, pop," I repeated softly.

He wrenched free of my grasp. "I can't get you no lawyer, boy." He shook his head as if to clear it. "They'd skin me alive—" He left the cell and closed the door behind him. "You think I got nothing better to do than to set here all afternoon talking to a man who's in jail for cutting a woman's throat? You think I got nothing better to do than that?"

"George!" I heard one of the deputies bawl.

"Yes, sir!" the old man answered. "Coming."

I lay back on my bunk. I was feeling better, stronger, but I felt that I must somehow preserve what strength I had to meet whatever might be coming next. Another trip to that room with Loy Bailey and his deputies would be hard to take. I'd known that even before the old man had warned me. A man could take just so much. I wouldn't sing any false tunes for Bailey and his boys as long as I knew what I was doing. But they obviously had ways of washing the truth from a man's mind.

I lay there, half dozing, thinking my muddled thoughts. Where, I wondered, was Ringo? Where was Gloria—and what did she think of me now? And Billy Ringo. Had she been waiting for me when she had been killed? Or had someone brought her there, forced her there, and then killed her? I couldn't forget the sight of her lying there, the warm sweet-sickish smell of her blood. I'd seen death before—plenty of it. But I'd never gotten over the horror of the look of it or the smell of it.

On Guadalcanal I had seen infantrymen throw dead Japanese into mudholes in the road to get temporary traction for the wheels of their jeeps. I still woke up nights hearing the sucking, crunching sound of rubber treads on decomposing flesh, seeing death as it was in the tropics, its face swollen to Mongoloid proportions, the pus-like matter of decay oozing from between its lips.

My thoughts wandered. Sam Foster. Sam and his letter from the Committee of Twelve. I'd let Sam down. When was it he'd been told to leave town, leave the county? August the sixth? When was that? Yesterday? The day before yesterday? Today? I'd lost track of time. Time was an endless machine grinding out seconds and minutes and hours and days and it made little difference to me. I'd let Sam Foster down. I'd tried to help him but I'd let him down and it really didn't matter. I'd let myself down, and that mattered more. My thoughts sucked and oozed and dragged through the mud of my mind. Where was Dusty now? What would Dusty think if she could see me now, in jail in a friendless town, charged with murder? What would she think? What would she say?

I closed my eyes and sleep curled the edges of my thoughts and I could see Dusty, see her clearly. Her eyes were knowing, her slim figure elegant. Her dress was black and very chic. In those days it had seemed to me that most of the women on Fifth Avenue between Fifty-Sixth Street and Sixty-First Street, between five and six o'clock on any weekday afternoon, had been slim, black-clad—and the most beautiful, exciting girls in the world. And Dusty had been one of the most seductive of them all.

I remembered. I remembered the rodeos and the fights at Madison Square and I remembered the pro football games at the Polo Grounds. And I remembered the shrieks of delight and the hard, cold glitter in her eyes as she watched the daring and the grace and the brutality of the riders and the fighters and the players.

I remembered, specifically, a Sunday afternoon at the Polo Grounds—The Giants versus the Green Bay Packers. We had been married a month.

"Like it?" I'd asked her.

"Love it."

"I thought you'd like it. I thought you'd like it for a change."

"We've been spending too much time indoors."

"Don't minimize the importance of being indoors," I told her.

Dusty tossed her head and looked sidewise at me with that it's-our-beautiful-secret expression that she had learned in her first and only year at the American Academy of Dramatic Arts. "It's wonderful indoors, too, darling," she said softly.

She seemed to be waiting for me to say something, and, just to make her stop looking like a perfume ad right there in the grandstand, I kidded her a little. "Football is only incidental. If it wasn't for frustrated women there'd be no football."

"You and your theories," Dusty said happily.

"It's like war," I said.

"You're crazy—"

"You remember seeing newsreels of the German women at Nazi mass meetings, don't you? Did you ever look at the eyes of those women? Have you ever seen naked cruelty and frustration and madness?"

"We're at a football game, darling. And stop talking about women. You'd think women were really responsible for wars."

"I wouldn't say they were responsible for wars. But I will say they enjoy them. With the exception of most of the mothers and some of the wives, they enjoy them. The excitement, the nervous tension, the quick parties and the quick marriages. Red Cross and Nurse's Aid and benefits and heroes and silent suffering and fun and excitement."

"Watch the game, darling."

I glanced at the field and saw that the Giants were lining up to try a field goal from Green Bay's forty yard line. Then I looked at Dusty as she watched and waited for the play. I had my own private theory about the relationship between a woman's sexual drive and the flare of her nostrils. Dusty's nostrils were wide.

She caught her breath as the ball sailed between the goal posts. "Those wonderful guys," she breathed. "Those sweethearts!"

I grinned. Dusty was lovely. The slim girls, the long-legged, black-clad girls. Dusty was one of them, and she was mine. I could hardly wait for the game to end so we could go back to the apartment on Fortieth Street. I would light a fire in the fireplace. Dusty and I would have a couple of highballs while the charcoal was preparing. Then I would put the steaks on while Dusty was tossing the salad. And then I would break out a bottle of Chianti. We'd have some music, some easy talk, and then we would go to bed early, and it would be all very nice and peaceful.

I reached for Dusty's hand and I pressed it; it was cold, and I could feel all the bones in it, and for some strange reason I shuddered.

When I woke up the lights were on in the cell blocks and I was amazed to discover that I had slept the afternoon away and that it was now almost night. I sat up on my bunk and I felt my face and lips. The swelling and soreness were almost gone, and my eyes no longer ached with fever. I stood and my legs were no longer rubbery. A desperate compulsion to get out of there, to start striking back at the people who had hurt me, was growing in me. I grabbed the bars and squeezed them until my knuckles got white and my forearms knotted, and the urge to get out of there grew until I could hardly breathe.

And then, through the barred window, came a sound that puzzled me. I stood quietly listening to it. It was like the hum of a swarm of bees—a round and swelling sound, growing louder, more immediate, as I listened. And then, as it grew closer, the pattern of the hum changed, and I recognized, though I could not understand, the excited, shouted voices of men.

And then the old jailer burst excitedly into the cell block.

"Hear that, boy?"

"Yes."

"Know what it is?"

I think I knew, at that point, what it was; but I would not, could not, bring myself to face the truth. "No."

"It's a mob! It's the first mob I've seen in Cartersville in eleven years!" The old man was beside himself with excitement. "It started forming an hour ago, out at Haley's packing house, outside of town, and it's growing, and it's headed this way, boy!"

"For me?" I asked.

"Hell, no! This mob don't want white meat! This mob wants black meat! Yankee nigger by the name of Sam Foster has gone and raped a white woman. Young woman, pretty. Virgie Lupfers, her name is!"

Chapter Thirteen

The old man turned and left me and the door to the cell block closed behind him. I stood there for a moment listening to the ugly, swelling sound of the mob, and Sam Foster's words—spoken without fear but with weariness, hopelessness, finality—came back to me:

"They killed Harry Moore and his wife at Mims on Christmas Eve of 1951. They put a bomb under his house and they killed Harry Moore right out and his wife died later in the hospital. Mims is seventy miles from here, Mr. Dolan."

And I remembered Ringo, weeks earlier, as he had paced the floor of his office, his hands clenched into fists, his great eyes gleaming like some mad prophet's.

I remembered the way he had looked and the things he had said:

"You've got to understand that I love these people. And because I love them I understand them.... I've got something special in mind for Sam Foster, if he doesn't stop breeding unhappiness out there ..."

And then I remembered Loy Bailey's words, the ones he'd spoken early that morning, the words he hadn't thought I'd heard:

"... It's going to be a busy day. And I'm going out to Ringo's fishing lodge tonight. There's pretty apt to be some exciting things going on around town tonight ..."

The mob was in town now, headed west for the quarters, and the sound that it made now was an angry, senseless sound, like the hysterical yappings of small dogs. And as I listened the sound grew fainter, fainter, as the group of men passed through town— crossed the park, I figured—then poured west down Central toward the quarters, and soon the sound that it made was again the swelling sound of a swarm of bees.

And I knew Sam Foster would be there, waiting for them, because it wasn't in him to run away.

I knew I had to get out of there. I didn't stop to think what might happen to me if I faced that mob. I only knew that I had been part and parcel of the rottenness that had instigated this riot and that if I didn't do something to try to stop this lynching I would be running from the thought of it as long as I lived.

I lost my head. I lunged at my cell door until my breath left me, and I slumped, hanging to the bars, sobbing with weakness and frustration. And then the old jailer was standing at my cell door.

His voice was kind. "No need to tear yourself apart, boy. I told you those men are after the nigger."

"Let me out of here, pop. I've got some money. Five thousand dollars. It's—"

He interrupted me. "You figure it's a good time to get away, huh, boy? Sheriff out of town. Everybody but the deputy on duty here on their way out to see the lynching." He shook his grizzled old head. "No, boy. Like I said, I ain't amounted to much all my life. But I ain't yet took a bribe."

"You know Sam Foster, pop?"

The old man nodded slowly. "Good nigger, I'd always thought. I'm mighty surprised Sam Foster'd go and do a thing like that. Rape a white woman. Even the niggers got no sympathy for one of their people that would go and do a thing like that."

"You know who this white woman is? This Virgie Lupfers?"

He shook his head.

"She's one of Adele's whores, pop. One of Ringo's whores!"

That stopped him for a moment. Then, "That don't make no nevermind. She's white, ain't she?"

"Where is the girl?"

"Nobody seems to know."

"Who said she'd been raped?"

"She did, the girl. Loy Bailey had her outside, in his car, and he called some of the loafers over to his car. I wasn't there to hear what the girl or Bailey said, but I heard one of them deputies spreading the word out under the rubber tree. Said the girl had a flat tire out on that back road coming in from Turkey Branch. Said she'd got out to change the tire and Sam Foster came driving on by. Said Sam stopped and offered to help her and the girl took him up on it, offered to pay him. Said Sam changed the tire, all right, and then when she went to pay him, he grabbed her, taken her out behind a palmetto patch, and raped her. Hot almighty, damn! Say, she's a real good-looking young woman—built like a brick outhouse!"

"Damn it, pop—wake up! Don't you know who's behind this?"

"Quieten down, boy! There's no need to shout."
He craned his neck toward the cell-block door. "I ain't
saying I'll believe a word of it," he said cautiously,
"but who?"

"Ringo."

He stared at me.

I talked quickly, desperately, because I knew now
that the old man was my only chance. I told him how
Ringo had sent me out to warn Sam Foster, and I told
him what Sam had told me when I had warned him. I
told him about the letter Sam had gotten warning him
to be out of town by sundown August sixth—
yesterday—or else. I told him what I'd overheard Loy
Bailey say about getting out of town tonight because
of what was going to happen. And then I asked him a
direct question:

"Do you think I killed Billy Ringo?"

"No, boy," he said, and his voice sounded weary.

"Then, by God—"

He interrupted me. "No, boy," and he shook his
head slowly and his thin old body sagged, and I was
suddenly aware of how old, how defeated, he really
was. "No. I can't help you. I'm an old man. I been a
fool all my life. Maybe you did kill her. Maybe you're
lying to me about Sam Foster. No. There ain't a thing
you could do anyhow. They're too strong for you.
They're too strong for all of us. There ain't a thing you
could do."

I said quietly, "I'll get Ringo for you, pop."

His body straightened. "How?"

"I don't know. But I'll get him!"

He fumbled in his pocket for keys. I watched him,
afraid to breathe. He reached a key toward the lock.
Then his body sagged again. He dropped the hand that
held the key. "No. I'm an old man. It's all I got, this
job. I can't do it, boy. I can't do it—" The door to the
cell block was not quite closed. Through the crack in

the door came a rasping, shouting voice. I thought I recognized it as Mallie's.

"George! Goddamn it, George—where are you?"

The old man stared dully at the floor. He did not answer.

"When I call for you, old man, you want to come a'running!"

The old man's body straightened again and he squared his shoulders.

"Yes, sir!" he shouted, and his voice was strong.

He turned quickly and opened the door to my cell. He stepped through the door. "The door'll lock when it's closed. I was bringing you water and you jumped me!"

I nodded.

He took the .38 Special from the worn holster at his hip and handed it to me.

"For Ringo," he said.

I squeezed his thin old shoulder. Then I turned, stepped through the cell door and left him.

The cell block door creaked angrily as I swung it open. Mallie was sitting at a desk opposite the door. He was reading a newspaper. As the door creaked he said, "Now goddamn it, George, when I—" and then he saw me standing in the doorway grinning at him and he saw the .38 leveled at his chest and his jaw dropped open and the cigar stub he held between his yellow teeth dropped to the desk in a flurry of sparks and ashes.

"Keep your hands on the desk, Mallie," I said.

His mouth worked as if he were trying to say something but he had lost his power of speech.

I crossed the room to him, still grinning.

"I'm glad you proved to me that a good cigar butt can come in handy, Mallie," I said. "I really am. Hold out your hand, Mallie."

His face paled.

"Hold it out like a good boy, Mallie," I said. I kept the gun leveled at his fat belly.

He stared at me, then turned one hand over slowly, palm up, on the desk. The slimy butt on the desk was still burning. I picked it up, blew on the lighted end until it glowed red, then ground it into his palm.

He screamed.

When the scream had trembled into moans, I said, "You're a noisy bastard, aren't you, Mallie? I can't stand that kind of noise. It gets on my nerves. I'm the high-strung, nervous type, Mallie. I'd just as soon fill that ugly pot-gut of yours full of lead as not. That's the way I am—impulsive. Stand up."

He got up, still moaning.

"Step out here, Mallie."

He stepped out, shakily, from behind the desk. I frisked him. He was clean.

"All right. I know you've been getting reports. Have they got Sam Foster yet, Mallie?"

He shook his head.

"They haven't had time to get to the quarters yet, is that it, Mallie?"

He nodded.

"I'm going to ask you to do a couple of little favors for me, Mallie. You like me well enough to do a couple of favors for me, don't you?"

He nodded.

"Pick up the telephone. Ask the operator for the Federal Bureau of Investigation in Miami. It's all right. They're in all the phone books. Anybody can call them."

He did as he was told.

While the operator was putting the call through I gave him his instructions. "Tell them you're a deputy sheriff of Carter County—that you're calling for your boss, who's out of town. Tell them a mob has formed here, that it's completely out of hand, and that there's going to be violence—either a race riot, a lynching, or both! Ask them to get somebody up here—quick. Tell them we'll meet them—if we're able to—at the junction of the main highway and highway 606, six miles east of town. You tell them that, Mallie."

Mallie's voice broke as he spoke. "You're crazy, Dolan. They won't come. They'll tell me to—"

I spoke quickly. "They'll come, Mallie. You'd be surprised how interested the F.B.I. is in things like this. They've been investigating the Harry Moore killing at Mims for months. They've been looking into the synagogue and colored real estate bombings in Dade County, too. It's been in the papers, Mallie; I'm surprised you haven't seen it. They'll be real interested in what's going on up here, Mallie. They might figure it to tie in with those other things. And for all I know, it might, at that!"

The sweat was pouring off Mallie's face. "Bailey'll kill me, Dolan. And if he don't, then Ringo will!"

I nudged his fat belly with the muzzle of the .38. "My nerves, Mallie. You don't want to forget my nerves."

The connection was made. Mallie started blurting out his business and was put through to a man named Carlton. I was standing close enough to Mallie to smell the stale wet stink of him and I could hear Carlton in Miami. He didn't sound especially happy when Mallie made his request.

"Why can't you people handle it?"

I whispered to Mallie, "The sheriff's out of town and you're understaffed."

Mallie repeated this to Carlton.

"What started your riot?"

"Nigger raped a white woman," Mallie replied.

I shoved the muzzle of the .38 three inches into the soft fat of his belly. "He's been *accused* of it," I whispered. "You don't believe it."

Mallie clutched at the desk for support. His face was ash-colored. "That is, they *say* he did. I—we don't believe it."

"You got the man in your jail?"

"No, sir."

"My God, man! Get him. Hold on to him! That's *your* job. If there's a violation of his civil rights, then it's my job. We'll be there as quickly as we can drive it. And I hope, for your sake, that you've been leveling with us! Can you meet us?"

I nudged him again with the .38. His eyes rolled and I was afraid, for a moment, that he was going to faint.

But he got it out. "Junction of the main highway into town and highway 606."

Carlton hung up and Mallie fumbled his receiver to its cradle. "I'm all through. It's like I'm dead already," he groaned.

"Get going," I said.

"Where to?"

"Sam Foster's house. In a big hurry!"

Mallie groaned again.

I stuck the .38 out of sight in a pants pocket, kept my hand on it, and followed Mallie through a door at the side. Two of the sheriff's office sedans were parked directly outside the door. I checked the first one for keys.

They were there. I nudged Mallie into the driver's seat and climbed in beside him. I cradled the .38 in my lap.

"Crank this heap and goose it," I said. "And I hope, for your sake, that we're not too late. I don't think my nerves could stand it!"

We heard the disordered sound of the mob before we saw it. And then we were behind it and we saw the road thronged with milling men—all of them, luckily, afoot. Some of them were armed—with shotguns for the most part—and some small boys scampered excitedly beside them.

It was the first mob I had ever seen. I had expected some hint of a measured tread of doom, an inexorable march of grim and determined men. There was none of this. From what I could see, there was no order, no authority; they simply swarmed, in a confused, slightly drunken, ragged way down the road. The sounds of rebel yells and shrill laughter and shouted obscenities accompanied them. The cohesive agent that held this mob together was hysteria; the men in it were on an emotional binge. And they were dangerous.

In spite of myself I shuddered.

We were less than a half mile from the quarters now. There was a road to the right and I had Mallie take it. Then we swerved left and came into the pot-holed clay roads of the quarters from the north. The streets were deserted, doors were shut, and windows were shuttered or blanked with shades. No cars were in sight: the people had gone or they were hiding in their houses. I wondered, momentarily, if Sam Foster had gone with them. I didn't wonder long. We slid to a hurried stop in front of Sam's house. Sam's living room was lighted. No shades were drawn. Sam sat in an easy chair in his living room. He was alone with his courage and his dignity, and he was waiting.

"Get in there," I told Mallie.

I didn't bother to knock. The door was unlatched and I threw it open, shoved Mallie through it, and followed him into the room. Sam rose. He looked at me and he said calmly, "I might of known it. I might of known you'd come, Mr. Dolan."

"It was close. And it'll get closer. Why did you wait, Sam?" I said. "You knew they were coming for you. The rest of your people knew. I've seen the houses—doors closed, shades drawn. You've told me that your people know about things in this county almost as soon as they happen. You knew this mob was coming for you. Why did you wait?"

I knew just about what he was going to say. But I
wanted to hear him say it. The sad-eyed man had a way
of showing me things that I hadn't known, or had
forgotten. Important things, things that I needed to
know.

"A man's got to face up to a thing, that's all. I'm
not anxious to die. But I don't care a thing in this world
about running out on a bad situation. If I wasn't here
when that mob got here they'd take it out on my
people. It'd be like it was in Groveland. The houses
would burn and there'd be shooting and innocent
people would die and there'd be misery. A man ain't
any kind of a man if he don't think first of them that
need him, Mr. Dolan."

"They need you alive, Sam."

"I was going to tell 'em I didn't do anything to that
girl, Mr. Dolan. I was going to tell 'em, if they'd let me
talk."

"Let me handle it, Sam. Stop being a martyr and let
me handle it! If they think you're innocent they won't
bother your people. Is that what you figure?"

He nodded eagerly.

"You won't get away with it, Dolan!" Mallie said.

I wheeled on him.

"They'll take you both, Dolan," he shouted.
"They're coming now. Hear 'em? They'll take you
both!"

I gave him the back of my hand across his loose
face. He fell back. "Listen, you fat bastard—and listen
good!" I told him. "You've got one chance of living to
see the light of day. One chance! You're going to do
something you'd never have the guts to do without this
gun to persuade you. You're going out on that front
porch and you're going to face that bunch of maniacs
and make a little speech. Sam Foster and I are going to
be with you. You're going to tell them that there's been
a couple of big mistakes. You're going to tell them that
there wasn't any rape—that the girl was drunk when

she told her story and when she came out of it she admitted that she'd dreamed the whole thing up. She'd been buying bolita tickets from Sam, here, and she'd been losing more than she could afford and she and Sam had had some kind of an argument over money and she'd decided to get even with him.

"They'll ask you about me. You're going to tell them that your office let the word get around that I'd killed Billy Ringo so Bailey could catch the real killer with his pants down. And that Bailey nabbed the killer this afternoon and has a signed confession from him. When they want to know who it is, tell them you're not at liberty to say—that this information will have to come from Loy Bailey, himself. If anybody asks you what I'm doing here with you and Sam, you'll tell them I've been deputized by your office to help you see to it that an innocent man does not become a victim of mob violence. Have you got that, Mallie? Have you got it all?"

Mallie's face was greenish-white. "You won't get away with it, Dolan! You don't know these people like I know 'em. They're geared for blood. They're gonna get it—one way or the other. They'll know I'm lying to them. They'll take you both—and me, too. Listen, Dolan. Take the car, take Foster—make a run for it. But don't make me face them boys with a pack of lies like that!"

I grabbed his wet shirt and I brought his face close enough to mine to smell the foul breath of him and I said, "You'll do what I said. You'll do it, by God, and you'll do it good, or you'll be dead!"

We could hear them now at the end of the road. I loosened my grip on Mallie's shirt.

"Ready, Sam?" I asked.

"I'm ready, Mr. Dolan."

"If it doesn't work, we'll run for it."

"If it don't work, there's no use running," Sam said.

I forced a grin. "I'm afraid you're right."

"Mr. Dolan," Sam said slowly, "how come you're doing this for me?"

"Maybe I'm not doing it for you, Sam. Maybe I'm doing it for myself. I'm in a jam, too, you know. The F.B.I. is on its way up here, Sam. They wouldn't have come to help me, but they're coming to help you. Maybe I figure if I can clear you I can clear myself at the same time. We're both bucking the same head wind, you know, Sam."

Sam nodded thoughtfully. "Maybe you're doing it for yourself, you say." He looked at me. "Maybe you're doing it for yourself in a way you don't exactly realize, Mr. Dolan. An inside sort of a way. Mr. Dolan, I'd like to shake your hand."

We clasped hands.

"I always did say your heart and your tongue didn't meet."

"They've come a lot closer in the last twenty-four hours, Sam."

Sam was quiet for a moment. Then he said softly, "They're about out in front now, Mr. Dolan."

I put the .38 slowly into my right pants pocket. "I'll be standing on your left, Mallie," I said. "And I'll be standing close. There won't be more than ten inches between you and the business end of this gun. Keep thinking of that, Mallie."

Mallie stared at me.

"Make a good speech, Mallie. Make a real good one. Let's go."

I'd timed it well. The first ten or twelve men in the ragged column were milling onto Sam's lawn. Mallie stepped through the front door onto Sam's porch. I followed him and Sam followed me. The men on the lawn stopped, slack-jawed at the sudden turn of events. They were silent for a moment. Then one of the men— I recognized him as the tall, lean mechanic, the first man I had spoken to in Cartersville—spoke: "We want the nigger, Mallie. We don't want no trouble from you. We want the nigger and we want him now."

Mallie's voice trembled as he spoke: "Hold off, boys—there's been a mistake."

The lean mechanic seemed to be the designated— perhaps self-designated—spokesman. "What's the white man doing here, Mallie? Ain't that the man that killed Ringo's wife?"

"We'll take 'em both!" somebody shouted. "A double feature!"

A man laughed shrilly.

The thickening crowd surged forward, yards closer to the porch. My skin prickled with fear as I moved closer to, and a little behind, Mallie. I whispered to him, my lips barely moving, "Stop 'em, Mallie. You'd better stop 'em. My nerves—"

Mallie's jowls glistened with sweat. He raised his hand over his head. "You boys don't want to go and do anything you'd be sorry for later," he said. "You know the way Loy Bailey and all of us boys down at the sheriff's office have always operated. We've always tried to give the people of Carter County what they wanted, even if it has meant closing our eyes to a few things and not going exactly by the letter of the law. I wouldn't stand between you boys and this nigger here if there hadn't been a mistake. There ain't been no rape, boys. That's the whole thing in a nutshell. The Lupfers girl was drunk. She'd been buying bolita tickets from the nigger here and she'd been losing heavy. They'd had some sort of a fuss over money. Had a grudge against him, I reckon. Anyway, when she sobered up she told us she'd dreamed the whole thing up."

"You're lying to us, Mallie," the lean mechanic said. "The girl! Where's the girl? Let's hear her story!"

Mallie groaned. "I don't know where the girl is, boys. We—we turned her loose. I don't know where she is."

"Git him!" somebody shouted. "The black sonofabitch thinks he's as good as a white man, anyhow. Git him!"

"We'll learn him!" another shouted.

I glanced at Sam. He stood there on his porch, calm, unmoving, his eyes fixed on a point above the shouting crowd, his features composed.

The lean mechanic held up a hand for silence.

"The white man, Mallie. Dolan. You ain't told us about Dolan."

Mallie's voice quavered. "We—we had to pull kind of a fast one on you there, boys. Or Loy did. We had to pick up Dolan, here, and let the word get around the county that he'd killed Mr. Ringo's wife. We figured the real killer would maybe tip his hand then. And he did, boys. That's the reason Loy Bailey ain't here to tell you these things himself. He's been busy. He picked the killer up earlier this evening and he's already got his signed confession."

The crowd murmured angrily. The mechanic's voice was edged with disbelief. "Who was it, Mallie? Who killed Ringo's wife?"

Mallie said lamely, "I can't tell you, boys. That's Bailey's order. That information will come from the sheriff himself, when he's ready to give it."

"Who? We want to know who!" shouted somebody. "Who was it, Mallie!"

"We got a right to know who!"

"He's lying in his teeth!"

Mallie sounded on the verge of tears. "I'm doing the best I can, boys. Give a man a break! I'm just a man working for a living, trying to get along. Give a man a break, boys!"

The mechanic faced the noisy mob. "Quiet, Goddamn it! Let's get to the bottom of this thing!" He turned to face Mallie. "What's he doing here, Mallie? What's Dolan doing here?"

Mallie choked his words out: "Because he's a special deputy. He's been sworn in as a special deputy of Carter County, by God, and he's here to help me!"

The mob received this with that seemed to be almost complete disbelief.

"He's lying!"

"Take 'em! Take 'em both!"

"Where's Bailey? We want to hear this from Bailey!"

The men in back surged angrily forward, pushing the men in front closer to the porch and I knew that our lives—Sam Foster's and mine—hung in the balance. If the front line broke, the whole mob, surging like flood waters through a ruined dike, would sweep us away. They didn't believe Mallie, but he had sown the seeds of doubt. I had one chance left and I took it. I palmed the butt of the .38 and I held it loosely before me and my finger caressed its trigger. I grinned at them.

"Most of you know who I am, boys," I said. "I work for Ringo. Ringo doesn't want any violence here tonight. I was deputized to help see that there is none. Mallie's done the talking. He's told you the truth. I'm here to back that truth up with lead if it becomes necessary. We're leaving now, boys—Sam Foster, Mallie, and I. I hope there won't be any trouble."

I had never bluffed for bigger stakes.

The crowd was silent.

"You first, Sam. Then Mallie. Go to the car."

Sam walked slowly down his front porch steps. Mallie stumbled in his wake. I followed Mallie. Sam led the way diagonally across his little lawn. Sam, then Mallie, then I, passed within four feet of the wall of men. Those few minutes seemed agonizingly long. I kept my eyes glued to the middle of Mallie's bobbling back as we crossed the lawn. Sweat poured from my armpits and ran cold against the sides of my belly, and my knees were rubbery. The rasping, tension-choked breathing of the men in the mob was the only sound.

My belly tightened as the wall of men seemed momentarily to waver, to strain forward. The acrid smell of stale sweat and eating-tobacco and sour mash whisky was overpowering in the hot air. Then Mallie stumbled, almost fell. As he regained his balance, I fought down a desperate compulsion to break and run for it.

And then, finally, Sam reached the car. He opened the rear door and climbed slowly into the back seat. "The wheel, Mallie," I whispered. The wheel was away from us. Mallie opened the right door and worked his way across the seat and under the wheel. I sat beside him. I closed the door gently. "All right, Mallie," I whispered. The motor coughed once, then purred. Mallie slipped it into gear. The back third of the mob stood silently in the clay road. The men, sullen-faced, parted slowly to let us through. "Easy, Mallie, easy," I whispered.

And then we were through them and around the first corner, out of their sight, and the car wavered, then coasted to a stop beside the road as Mallie slumped, moaning, at the wheel. "I'm through," he moaned. "All through. It's like I'm dead already."

I hurried out of the car, around it, and, with Sam's help, I muscled Mallie's dead weight to the right of the front seat. I shoved the butt of the .38 at Sam. He took it.

"I don't think he'll start anything—but watch him!"

I goosed the car toward town, nosed onto the main highway and headed east for its junction with 606.

It promised to be a busy evening.

Chapter Fourteen

Sam's watch made it nine forty-five. And, though it seemed like hours, I knew it couldn't have been much more than forty-five minutes since Mallie had talked with the F.B.I. man, Carlton, in Miami. It was something less than sixty miles from the junction to Miami. With big city traffic to contend with at the start, I figured another forty minutes, at least, before Carlton would arrive. I wanted Sam with me—there was no telling when that mob might start feeling frustrated enough to go gunning for him again—but Mallie was a problem. I wanted Carlton to have facts, not fiction, when he arrived. And Mallie would be of no help there. I was afraid to let him go; he knew where Carlton was expecting to be met. And he could—if he managed to pull himself together—louse up my plans completely.

I pulled to a stop at the side of the highway. I slid from under the wheel and opened the trunk. Among the tools and odds and ends I found a stretch of inch-and-a-half towline. Too heavy, but the strands would separate. I dragged the line from the trunk and piled it into the back seat. "Got a knife?" I asked Sam. He nodded. "Peel off a strand of this. Get me eight or ten yards and cut it in half." Sam nodded and went to work. I drove on, slowly. A clay road left the highway and disappeared in a grove of live oaks. I took it, drove several hundred yards, then stopped again.

"Anybody live around here?" I asked Sam.

"Not as I know of, Mr. Dolan."

Mallie was still huddled in a loose heap by my side. "Outside, Mallie," I said.

"Please, Mr. Dolan," he blubbered. "I done like you asked me to, didn't I? I stood up there in front of the boys and I dug my own grave with my mouth, didn't I? You got no call to hurt me anymore. Just put me out yonder on the big road. That's all I'm asking you. Put me out yonder on the big road and I'll start walking and I won't stop till I'm out of Carter County!"

"Outside, Mallie," I repeated.

He got out, groaning. I followed him. He turned to face me. I grabbed a fat shoulder and spun him around. Sam handed me a stretch of rope. I tied Mallie's hands behind him. Then I stuck a foot in front of him, shoved, and dumped him to the ground. I tied his ankles together. He was sobbing now. "You can't leave me out here. You can't do it, Mr. Dolan. A man could die out here before somebody found him!"

"That's true, Mallie," I said. Sam got into the seat beside me. I backed, turned, and the rear wheels fought for traction as I churned out of there.

There were no cars at the junction of the main highway and 606. A hundred yards down 606, just off the road, was a crazily leaning, dilapidated barn. I pulled in behind it, parked the car so I could see the junction, doused the lights, and waited. After a moment Sam said patiently, "What we waiting for, Mr. Dolan?"

It occurred to me that Sam had been told nothing. "This is where we meet the F.B.I., Sam," I said.

He thought for a moment. "You been accused of murder and I been accused of rape. We both been working for Mr. Ringo. You reckon that government man will listen to us, Mr. Dolan?"

"He'll listen because he's got to listen. And he'll give us a chance to prove we're right. One chance. And we've got to make it good."

"You got a plan, Mr. Dolan?"

"I've got a plan."

I said nothing more and Sam didn't push me. We waited. The minutes dragged endlessly by, their arrival and departure accompanied by nervous drags of cigarette smoke and fretting, nagging thoughts. Sam and I were operating on borrowed time—and it wouldn't last forever. Somebody—Bailey or one of his other deputies—would find Pop in my cell. The alarm would go out. We'd be hunted down, Sam and I, and this time we wouldn't stand a chance.

I chain-smoked, and mentally cursed the inefficiency of all Federal bureaus, and most especially the Federal Bureau of Investigation. My fists clenched with nervousness as cars slowed at the junction, made the turn, then sped away through the night. I didn't think I could stand it much longer. Maybe the alarm had gone out already. Maybe they were on the way out from town now, carloads full of them, armed to the teeth and spoiling for the kill. I wondered if we should run for it, try and make Miami. Maybe ...

The lights of another car, traveling fast from east to west, swept into view. I watched the lights, saw the car slow as it approached the junction, then swerve from the highway to the sloping, grassy shoulder beside it and jerk to a stop. I felt my whole body go tense. I watched the car. The headlights blanked and the parking lights went on. A man climbed from under the wheel, checked the highway sign, then walked in front of the lights. I knew the time had come for me to do some fast talking. I started the sedan, pulled around the old barn and onto 606.

"Good luck, Mr. Dolan," Sam said.

"We'll need it," I said.

I pulled to a stop ten yards from the other car and got out.

"Carlton?" I called.

"That's right." Carlton was my own age, perhaps a few years older. Dapper in a tan suit and light felt hat. Small, thin, wiry—with tight lips and hard eyes. There were two men with him—one in the front seat, the other in the back. "You the deputy that called?"

"No," I said.

"Then where in hell is the—"

I interrupted him. "We haven't much time. You've got to listen to me. I'll level with you—right from the start. Let me finish and then I'll answer your questions."

Carlton waited, his eyes narrow, wary.

"My name is Dolan. An hour and a half ago I was in jail in Cartersville—accused of murdering a woman named Billy Ringo."

Carlton's right hand snaked beneath his open jacket toward the bulge beneath his left shoulder.

"Got it, Tom," the man in the back seat drawled— and I looked into the muzzle of a .45.

"Relax," I said. "I'm clean. There's a .38 in the front seat of my car if you want it."

"Who's the man in your car?" Carlton asked.

"That's a friend of mine named Sam Foster. He's the man you want to see. He's the man bucking the bum rape charge. He's the man the mob's been after."

Now Carlton's gun was in his hand. "Come out of there!" he shouted at Sam. "Come out of there with your hands high!"

The other men were out of the car. Sam stumbled into the circle of light, his hands high above his head, his face mournful. One of the men frisked him. Then he checked me. "Nothing," he grunted.

"Get the .38 in the car," Carlton said. "All right, uncle," he said to Sam, "drop your hands." He turned to me. "Start talking. And you'd better talk good!"

I didn't pull any punches. I told them what I knew about the way the county was run and I didn't dodge the fact that Sam Foster and I had been knee-deep in the filth and rottenness of it. I knew that the F.B.I.'s interest was in the lynch threat, the violation of civil rights, but I was trying to wrap that and my murder rap in the same neat package and hand it to them. Carlton only interrupted me once, when I told him about the warning Sam had gotten.

"Can you show me that?" he asked.

Sam's face lighted. "Just so happens I got it right here."

I breathed a sigh of relief.

Sam fished in his billfold and came up with it. Carlton scanned it and stuffed it in a pocket. "Go ahead," he told me.

I finished my story. "That's it," I said.

"What do you think, boys?" Carlton asked.

They were both silent for a moment. Then one of them said, "If the guy's lying I don't get his pitch. If he really knocked this babe off, then broke jail, what's he doing playing footsie with the old guy, here? Hanging around the county, poking his neck out, when he could be making himself scarce?"

"And how come he got us up here?" the other asked.

Carlton stared at me for a moment with those cold eyes. "I'm not saying I'm buying your yarn, Dolan. I'm not saying that. But I'm going to give you a chance to prove it. So far we've heard one version of this melodrama—yours. I want another version. You say you've got the deputy who called me in Miami hobbled and hogtied back the road a piece. Let's go get him, Dolan. Let's listen to him talk. And if I still think there's a chance that you might be leveling I'll want to talk with the girl who is supposed to have claimed rape. Virgie. Virgie Whatshername."

"Lupfers. Virgie Lupfers."

"Think you can find her?"

"They've got her hidden out. I'm sure of that. But I think I can find her."

"We'll take both cars. We might need them. Joe, you drive our car and take the old guy with you. Harry and I'll ride with Dolan, here. Follow us. And stay close."

He turned to me. "Get in, Dolan. You drive. And don't pull anything that's not in the script. Let's go find that deputy."

I nosed down the clay road five minutes later. I pulled into the grove of oaks where Sam and I had left Mallie.

But Mallie was not there.

Those cold eyes were on me again. The voice was as thin and wiry as Carlton himself: "Well?"

I felt like a schoolboy caught cribbing an answer on an exam. "He was here," I said lamely. "Forty minutes ago he was here—"

"You've crapped out on your first roll, Dolan."

"He was here, I tell you."

"I don't know what you're trying to pull, Dolan. But I'm beginning to feel a little unhappy about the whole thing. I'm not a nice guy to be around when I'm unhappy, Dolan. I'm going to give you one more chance to make me happy. One more. Can you find me the girl, Dolan?"

He had me sweating. "I can find you the sheriff of this county, Carlton—if the man I left here hasn't gotten to a phone and warned him that all hell was breaking loose in town and that you people were on your way from Miami. I can find him and I can make him tell us where the girl is. It's a forty-five minute drive from here. Will you take a chance?"

He thought for a moment. "This time you'd better be right, Dolan."

The highway skirted town and we didn't stop. The speedometer wavered between ninety-eight and a hundred until I left the highway and slithered along the back country roads that led to Ringo's fishing lodge. I spoke once:

"Will you let me handle this my own way, if Bailey's there?"

Carlton thought it over. Then: "I've played along with you this far. I've promised you a chance to prove you're leveling. If that's the way you want it—then that's the way it will be. You start it. We'll finish it— one way or the other. If he's there—"

If he's there, if he's there ... The words beat against my brain with a throbbing, monotonous rhythm. *If he's there, if he's there* ... He *had* to be there!

The miles seemed endless. And then, finally, we reached the turn that pointed the road straight to the river and Ringo's lodge. I slowed the car to a crawl, blanked the lights, and made the turn. Ringo's lodge was less than half a mile straight away. The big front room was lighted. It could, I thought, be Preacher, the caretaker.

It wasn't until we were two hundred yards from the house and I saw Bailey's Mercury sedan that the tension that had churned my stomach and knotted the muscles of my arms and shoulders eased up.

"All right. He's here!" I told Carlton.

Carlton was staring at me. "Wait a minute," he said.

"I don't like that look on your face. Maybe I'd better—"

"Carlton," I said, "this is a man who has jailed me twice on false charges. This is a man who has beaten me with fists and wet towels and hoses. This is a man who has thrown hot coffee in my face. This is a man who has planned to kill me." Carlton winced as I tightened a hand on his arm. "This is *my* boy, Carlton—you promised—"

"All right!" he said. "All right! Try it your own way first. We'll be right behind you. But for God's sake take it easy!"

I grinned at him. I stopped the car halfway between the house and Ringo's cockpit. The F.B.I. car pulled up beside ours. I got out. One of the Feds still had Pop's .38. That was all right with me. I didn't want it.

A gun was too quick and impersonal a weapon to use on Loy Bailey. And besides that I didn't want him dead. I wanted him alive and I wanted him singing. Singing pretty. And the anticipation of the delightful chore that lay ahead of me was almost more than I could bear.

I made the front corner of the house, stepped noiselessly to the dock that ran along the front of the house; tried the door to the front porch, found it unlocked, and stepped from the dock to the porch. A radio was blaring jive. Through a window I could see the back of Bailey's bullet head and over his heavy shoulders I could see a card table. He was deep in a game of solitaire and I knew if I stood there watching him long enough I'd catch him cheating. Beside the cards on the table was his artillery—his gun belt and his holstered .45. Across the room, at the bar, I saw a woman building a drink. When she raised her head I saw that it was Adele.

It was obvious, from the open door, the lights, the blaring radio, the relaxed attitudes, that Bailey had had no warning from Mallie. I couldn't see the far end of the room but I felt reasonably sure that these two were the only ones in the room. I crossed the porch under the noise from the radio, leaned easily against the solid door between the porch and the front room, and slowly, very slowly, turned the knob, feeling for the pressure, the point of resistance, that would tell me it was locked.

The knob turned and the door cracked slightly as I leaned against it. I shouldered it wide open and stepped into the room and stood there, ten feet from Loy Bailey, grinning at him.

Adele screamed.

"You—" Bailey said, and he half stood, and the split second it took him to get his thoughts in gear and go for his gun was a split second too many. I aimed a foot at the card table and the cards flew and the gun thumped to the floor and when Bailey stooped, clawing for it, I brought a knee to his face and heard him grunt and felt teeth give and then saw him straighten and stare wildly at me as blood bubbled from the corner of his mouth.

He swung at me—a roundhouse right that a blind man could have seen coming—and I went inside it, pumping short jabs to his soft belly, and when he fell back, gasping, I raked his face with an outside-in right and felt flesh tear from his cheekbone as he went down in a pile.

And then a voice, a screaming voice, hysterical, drunken, or both—a woman's voice, not Adele's—came from the end of the room. "Kill him! Kill the bastard! Kill him, kill him!" I looked quickly toward the far end of the room and saw that the girl half-sitting, half-lying on the couch, her hair matted, her torn slip twisted about her thighs, her eyes wild and staring, was Virgie Lupfers.

Carlton had decided it was time to take over. He and his two pals, guns drawn, came through the door from the porch.

I fought for breath to speak. "All right, Carlton. This side of beef on the floor is the sheriff of Carter County. The woman behind the bar is his girl-friend and, incidentally, the madam of a first-rate cathouse. The kid on the couch is Virgie Lupfers. These gentlemen, my friends, are agents from the Federal Bureau of Investigation in Miami. They have a few questions they'd like answered. Like who was responsible for the rape charge against Sam Foster, just for instance."

"I'll run this show, Dolan," Carlton said. "I'll ask the questions."

I shrugged.

Virgie was sobbing. "Get me a drink. For God's sake get me a drink!" Carlton went to the bar, slopped a couple of fingers of bourbon into a tumbler, and took it to her. Virgie tossed it off, gasped, and put the tumbler on the floor. She ran a shaking hand through her hair in an abortive attempt to straighten it, smoothed her torn slip modestly around her thighs, and said, "There wasn't no rape. She made me say there was. Her, Adele! She *made* me say the nigger had raped me!"

Carlton fastened those cold eyes on Adele. "Talk, lady."

Adele was frightened. Her eyes were wide and her hand shook as she fumbled a cigarette from a package on the bar. "She's lying! Dirty whore lies! She's drunk and she doesn't know what she's saying!"

"You ever do any time on a white-slavery rap, lady?"

Adele couldn't get her match to light.

Carlton crossed to the bar, flipped a lighter, and held the flame to her cigarette. His face was close to hers and his words were spat through tight lips. "I asked you a question. I want an answer!"

Loy Bailey sat up, groaning. He slatted blood from his chin, tried to struggle to his feet, decided it was not worth the effort, and slumped back against the wall. Adele stared at him, her face sick with disgust.

"Well?" Carlton asked her.

"It was him!" she blurted, pointing to Bailey. "It was his idea, right from the start! He said he needed one of my girls for a special job. I didn't know what he wanted her for. Honest! It was him, that sorry excuse for a man there on the floor. I run a good, clean place. Everybody gets a square shake at Adele's. I've never been in any trouble. You can ask anybody!"

"You're in trouble now, lady," Carlton said.

Her voice was thick with hatred now. "I should have known. I should have known better than to trust him. He's a fool. He's always been a fool. A stupid, bumbling, thick-headed fool! I've played along with him because I thought he could help me. Him, help me! What a laugh!"

Bailey was staring at her with stricken eyes. His breath came in wet red bubbles. Carlton turned to him.

"What about it, mister?"

Bailey muttered. "Lies. All lies!"

"You'd better come clean, mister."

Bailey struggled to his feet and stood, swaying, shaking his head to clear it, and said, "By God, I'm the sheriff of this county. I've got some rights here, and I'll by God—"

I couldn't stand it any longer. At this rate we'd be here all night, and I had a little unfinished business to attend to. I knew Bailey was yellow and I knew how to get the truth out of him, and get it quick. I moved in on him, too fast for Carlton to stop me.

This time, I was holding the cards. His arms covered his face and I went for his belly again. He went backward, back against the wall, gasping, and his shoulders drooped and his heavy arms dropped to cover his midsection and I went to work on his face. It was like shooting a sitting duck, but I took a certain pleasure in it. Short, quick jabs—like a workout with a light bag. I worked over his eyes, closing them. I was thinking of the hoses, the coffee in my face. I felt his nose go, and I remembered the time he'd hit me, the first time, there in the cell, and I remembered the tobacco juice, and I laughed and moved to his lips, cutting them, splitting them. Bailey was making hoarse, grunting sounds now, hurt-animal sounds, and I hated to leave my work but I was afraid he couldn't take any more.

I stood away from him.

"Who rigged this thing? Who got the girl to lie?"

He was crying now, blubbering.

I moved toward him.

"No!" he blubbered. "No more. For God's sake, no more. I'll talk!"

Carlton moved in. "We're listening."

"Ringo," he said. "It was Ringo—it was his idea. He wanted Sam Foster out of the way. He made me do it. Made me get the girl, have her lie, then get out of town so the boys could take care of Sam Foster. I reckon they got him by now. But it was Ringo. Ringo, I tell you!"

"Foster's with us, Bailey. We've got Foster."

If Bailey heard this he made no sign of understanding it. He was babbling now. "Like Billy Ringo—that was Ringo, too! I had nothing to do with it. You go get Rand Ringo ..."

My hand was a vise on Carlton's arm. "Hear it, Carlton? Hear it?"

He nodded.

"Not Billy Ringo," Bailey moaned. "Not Billy! Ringo wanted me to take care of Billy and I wouldn't do it. I'm just a man trying to get along. Maybe I've been a little slack about a thing or two, but—"

I'd heard all I wanted to hear. Carlton and his boys were wrapping things up and tying them with a pretty red ribbon. They had all they needed on Bailey and Adele. The two of them were all through; they'd had it.

Now I had things to do on my own and I didn't want any interference. I edged toward the door. Nobody noticed me. I eased through the door, hit the dock at a dead run, and I didn't stop running until I reached the car I'd driven out from town. I slammed behind the wheel, started the car, whipped it backward, and then headed it back the way we'd just come. Sam Foster had gotten out of the other car. He was staring anxiously at me. "Mr. Dolan, what—"

"Later, Sam," I said. "It's all right. Later—"

I put a heavy foot on the accelerator and started wondering what sort of a reception I'd get at Ringo's house.

Chapter Fifteen

I had no definite plan as I left the highway and wheeled into the graveled drive that led to Ringo's house. Three-quarters of the way in from the highway I pulled off the drive and yanked the car to a stop behind a banyan. Beyond me was pasture. Obliquely across the pasture, less than half a mile away, I could see the lights of Ringo's house. The car was hardly hidden—for anyone who might be searching for strange cars—but it was the best I could do. I shinnied the whitewashed fence that bordered the pasture and started cross-country on a direct line for the house. The Brahman steers in the pasture regarded me with passive, unafraid eyes. With their moon-shot, glistening hides, their massive heads and their weirdly humped backs they reminded me of carved Oriental idols.

I left the pasture and skirted the stables behind the house. Sticking to the shadows as closely as possible, I made my way to the dressing room at the end of the swimming pool. As nearly as I could remember, this was directly opposite Ringo's study. The dressing room was a generous hundred yards from the house.

Lights shone dimly through bamboo-strip shades drawn across the windows of the study. I waited, watching the drawn shades, looking for moving shadows behind them that would tell me the room was occupied. I saw nothing. I thought of going to one of the windows and listening but discarded the idea. There was no shelter, no concealment, under the windows. I'd be a sitting duck for any stakeout Ringo might have decided to post around the house.

A shoulder-high hedge stretched from the corner of the dressing room to the garage at the rear of the house. I decided to try entering the house from the back; there was cover there, and none in front. I could only guess that Ringo was there, but I somehow felt certain that he was. I could only guess at how much he knew of my activities of the past several hours. But the chances were he'd been kept posted. He'd almost certainly know that I was on the loose, that the Sam Foster deal had backfired. And if Mallie Wilson hadn't hit the big road for parts unknown, Ringo would also know that the F.B.I. was interested in the Sam Foster fiasco. Ringo would know he was on a spot. And if he reacted as I was almost sure he'd react, he'd be dangerous. I was beginning to regret the half-cocked way I'd run out on Carlton and his pals. I didn't even have a gun, and I'd been pushing my luck long and hard that evening.

The hedge line ended two feet from the rambling, six-car garage. The slot nearest me gaped black and empty and I stepped into its welcome darkness to plan my next move.

"Mr. Dolan—" The sound behind me was almost a hiss. I felt my mouth go dry as I whirled.

The voice was frightened now. "Ain't nobody but me, Ben, Mr. Dolan. I don't mean you no harm—"

"What are you doing here?"

"I been waiting for you, Mr. Dolan."

"Waiting for me?"

"Yes, sir. You know, some folks think the colored can see in the dark. That ain't so. It's just that you don't hide yourself so good. I live right upstairs, here, right over the garage. I been waiting for you, watching. I seen you coming out of the pasture. I seen you go past the stables and on down by the pool. Then I watched you start on back here, behind the hedge. So I just come on down my stairs and waited for you here."

I shook my head to clear it. "You knew I was coming?"

"Sam Foster told me he figured you was. I got my own phone up there where I live at. Sam called me maybe thirty minutes ago. Woke me right up out of the bed. Told me he was worried about you, the way you went off, and all. Told me to watch for you and do what I could to see you didn't come to no harm."

"Sam's a friend of yours?"

"I reckon Sam's about the best friend I ever had, Mr. Dolan. Him and me spends lots of time together. We've spent lots of time talking about you, Mr. Dolan. What you did for Sam Foster tonight was nothing more than the kind of a thing Sam and me figured you might do."

I didn't have time to think about it. "Ringo's in there?"

"He's there, all right, Mr. Dolan. And he's acting mighty strange." My eyes were becoming accustomed to the pitch darkness of the garage. I could see the whites of Ben's eyes now. "Mighty strange! Ranting, roaring, stalking around the house, making speeches. He's mighty upset about you, Mr. Dolan. He knows you're a'loose. Says he hopes you show up here. Says after what you did to Miz Ringo there's nothing he'd rather do than meet you face to face."

"You say he's making speeches. Who's he making speeches to, Ben?"

"Miss Gloria. And another lady—one I never seen before."

"How can I get into the house, Ben?"

"I'll get you in."

I was silent and the old man sensed the question in my mind. "Because Sam Foster asked me to help ain't all!" he blurted. "It's Miss Gloria, mainly. He's evil, Mr. Ringo is! He'll ruin that girl just like he's ruined everybody else that's looked to him to be treated decent. I been seeing Mr. Ringo operate for a long time. I—"

"I think I understand, Ben."

"You better take this." Ben handed me an ancient .44 and the cool feel of it was good in my hand. "You follow me."

We stuck to the shadows, moved cautiously along the back of the house until we came to a tiled patio roofed with massed bougainvillea. French doors opened into the darkened living room. Ben fished in his pocket for keys and unlocked the doors. "He's most likely in his study," he whispered. "He'll be looking for you. Be careful, Mr. Dolan. Ain't nothing more I can do."

I made it to the door of Ringo's study without incident. Through the door I could hear music and the low sound of a woman's voice.

I held Ben's .44 lightly in my right hand. I breathed deeply, once, twisted the knob, and shouldered my way into the room. Gloria Ringo was across the room. She stifled a scream and stared at me with terror-stricken eyes. Ringo was not there. The woman on the other side of the room by the phonograph was long-legged, slender. Her wide mouth twitched as she looked at me. Her green eyes were wide with fear. Her makeup was heavy but it could not hide the lines of dissipation around her mouth or her eyes or the beginnings of slackness at the jaw line. She had changed a great deal since I had last seen her. And the changes had not been for the better. But I would have known her anytime, anywhere—she was Dusty Randall.

I stared back at her. I could hardly grasp the fact of her being here—in Rand Ringo's house.

Her voice was flat, colorless, tired. "It's been a long time, Brad. You've changed."

"Yes." I waited for the thing to hit me. I waited for the inevitable reaction: a shock, the pain of old wounds reopened; a softening, a hardening; a feeling of desire or of repulsion; of love or of hatred. I stood, tensed, staring at her, waiting for it to hit me, waiting for the conflicting emotions that had torn at me for years to consolidate, to jell, at the sight of her. I waited. And there was nothing! I was dead inside. Dusty Randall was a stranger. My lips twisted in a grin of self-mockery. I'd been riding a dream that was dead, and I'd been nursing a bitterness that didn't exist!

"I tried to tell you, Brad," Gloria said. "Last night, on the bluff above the river. I tried to tell you—and I couldn't do it. I was afraid—"

Last night! It seemed weeks ago. I remembered that she'd had something she wanted to tell me. And I remembered Ringo's reference—at his lodge, the night before the cockfight—to Dusty and our marriage. I remembered the mockery in his voice and the smugness in his face. And I remembered Gloria's concern for me then.

Gloria screamed, but it was too late. I felt the touch of steel in the small of my back. I cursed my stupidity. The shock of finding Dusty there had been too much for me. I'd asked for it and I'd gotten it. I was through. "Drop it, Dolan," Ringo said. The .44 thudded against the thick rug. Ringo prodded me away from it, picked it up, pocketed it, and walked backward keeping his Luger trained on my chest. He stood behind his desk and smiled politely at me.

"How nice, Dolan," he said. "We've been waiting for you. We had a phone call saying that you might drop by for a visit. One of Bailey's deputies."

I said quietly, "What are you going to do, Ringo?"

His voice was soft, polite. "I regret to say that I'm going to kill you, Dolan."

Gloria sobbed harshly.

Ringo's tone of voice changed and became sly, wary: "Hear the music, Dolan? Hear it? Tell me, Dolan. What is it? What is it?"

I listened. It was French orchestral music but I wasn't familiar with it. I shook my head.

Now his voice was triumphant. "You don't know?"

"No."

"It's Chabrier's *Marche Joyeuse*, Dolan. I told you I'd stump you. I told you, didn't I? And I have!" His voice was anxious now. "And Dusty Randall. Quite a shock finding her here, isn't it, Dolan?"

"No."

I almost felt sorry for him at that moment, again. "Damn you!" he shouted. "This woman is my mistress!"

"That's just barely interesting," I said.

He wouldn't let it go. He wouldn't accept the fact that it didn't matter to me. He wouldn't give it up. "I found out where she was, Dolan. I had friends trace her. I thought it might be amusing—even useful—to have her available. You know where I found her, Dolan?"

I shook my head.

"Miami Beach. Wasn't that convenient? I'm not surprised, however. Miami Beach is a mecca for ex-show girls and ex-models. There's a price on everything in Miami Beach. And the prices are high. Sort of a modern Babylon, Miami Beach—a city dedicated entirely to pleasure. Sunshine and sin. A twentieth century phenomenon."

His eyes gleamed wildly and his voice boomed. "Million dollar hotels built wall-to-wall almost on the edge of the primordial ooze of the Everglades. And it won't last, Dolan. It can't last! One day the grandfather hurricane of them all will cleanse it of its filth, and the 'Glades will creep up and suck its foundations into slime!"

"Quite a speech," I said. "And maybe you're right. You should be an authority on rottenness. And Miami Beach is where you found Billy, isn't it?"

His face darkened. His voice lowered. "You call a number, Dolan. A man comes to your hotel room to see you. It's all very businesslike. He has a briefcase. He shows you interesting pictures of girls. There is a short discussion of rates. You might be interested in knowing that your ex-wife's rates were quite high. But she's good. She's very good. She's so good that she works for me, now." He smiled at Dusty. "Don't you, darling?"

"You bastard," Dusty said.

I felt sick.

"I tried to tell you," Gloria repeated. "I knew he'd been seeing her in Miami. There were phone calls, letters left opened—I tried to tell you. She's never come here before, though—"

"Gloria, it doesn't matter. There's nothing staler than a dredged-up dream. I know that now. And where there's no love there's no hurt. That scar tissue you once said I was hiding behind—that's all gone, Gloria."

Ringo's voice was evil. "You haven't got long, Dolan."

I stood there, silent, tensed, watching his forefinger play nervously around the trigger guard of the Luger— waiting, steeling myself for the shock of the bullet, then the darkness. I wondered, incongruously, if I would hear the sound of the exploding powder first. *"You don't worry about the ones you can hear,"* we used to say in the Army. At this range, though, it might be different. But then, why should it be? The ratio between the sound of the exploding powder and the speed of the bullet would remain constant, wouldn't it?

My thoughts were chaotic. I couldn't arrive at a conclusion. There must be some simple algebraic formula. But then I was never very good at algebra, I reminded myself. I shook my head to clear it. I should do something—anything—even if it was wrong! I stared at that nervous finger, watching it now as it slipped inside the trigger guard and caressed the trigger; watching it as if it had hypnotic powers. *Do something!* I thought desperately. *Say something!*

"You won't get away with it, Ringo," I said.

He smiled pleasantly. "This is still my county, Dolan. I'm still calling the shots around here."

"But not for long."

"The F.B.I.? I'd heard that they might come. They've got nothing on me. They'll have nothing on me when I kill an escaped murderer in self-defense."

"They're here, Ringo. Here in your county! They've talked to Loy Bailey. Bailey has spilled his guts. You're all through, Ringo. You might have gotten away with murder. You might have gotten away with your gambling and your bootlegging and your whores and your political corruption for the rest of your life. But you went too far when you tried to frame Sam Foster, Ringo. Civil rights have been violated and you've been tagged as the instigator. That's a Federal offense, Ringo. And when they start probing for that particular rottenness the rest of the corruption is going to be uncovered. The stink will rise to the skies. You've got the Feds on your tail, Ringo, and you're all through!"

His face seemed frozen. "They'll never take me, Dolan. They'll never take me! Not here. Not in my county. I'm too strong for them. Too strong, do you hear! I've grown with this county, Dolan. The county's grown with me. I've always loved and understood the people of this county. I've always understood their weaknesses, their ambitions, their failures. They're my people, Dolan. I've always been like a father to them. My people will help me. They won't see me railroaded!"

His tone puzzled me. It was almost as if he spoke with sincerity. He couldn't really believe this. And yet—

"Loy Bailey, for one. I've had to be rather harsh with Loy at times. But Loy has always understood that it was for the best. He's grateful to me for all I've done for him. Loy would never turn on me, as you say he's done. You're wasting your time with lies like that, Dolan!"

"Ringo," I said, "Loy Bailey and Adele have been planning to take over this county for themselves!

You've been living on borrowed time! I've been saving that information for you. I was looking for you yesterday to give it to you. You were here, weren't you? But you wouldn't see me."

His laughter was high, shrill, mocking, unbelieving.

I was asking for it but I wouldn't stop. "They all hate you, Ringo! You can't rule by fear and not be hated. In your own small-time way you're as bad and as deluded as the big boys—Hitler, Stalin, Mussolini, and all the rest. Sure, they bow and scrape to you, Ringo. But they bow and scrape with hate in their hearts. And there's probably not a man in this county—though ninety-eight per cent of them would never admit it, even to themselves—who doesn't want you dead!"

Dusty's voice rose shrilly: "Get us out of here, Brad! He's crazy! He'll kill us all!"

"You asked for it, baby," I said. "And I guess I did, too."

Ringo's voice was sad, now. His body slumped. In other circumstances he would have seemed a pathetic figure. "You've all turned against me. Everybody's turned against me. I've been good to you all, haven't I? I've given you love, friendship, money.... You've all turned against me. Why? What have I done?"

"Billy," I said. "Just to mention one small thing. You killed Billy and then tried to pin the rap on me."

Gloria stifled a scream with two clenched fists and her eyes were wide with terror.

Ringo's body straightened and those great eyes shone and I knew then, knew once and for all, finally, that he was mad. "I killed her. Of course I killed her!" He pawed in a pocket with his free hand and came up with a slim, pearl-handled knife—the type that most of the citrus men in the area used to cut and sample fruit. He released the single, eight-inch blade, threw the knife, blade first, at his desk and it stuck there, quivering in the light. "I killed her with that. I found her in your house—my house—waiting for you, Dolan, and I killed her, and there's not a jury in the state that would convict me of it. Of course I killed her. I gave her everything—position, wealth, power! She was nothing when I found her, but I made her Mrs. Rand Ringo! But she turned against me. I knew how she felt about you, Dolan. I saw it coming. And after that cockfight I knew it. I knew she loved you. But she forgot one thing, Dolan. She forgot that nobody bucks Ringo and lives!"

"Like your first wife, Ringo? Like Bence, your partner?" It was a shot in the dark. Pop's suspicions could have been the idle meanderings of an old man's mind.

Ringo's face was evil now. The finger was nervous on the trigger again. I braced myself.

"You've gone too far, Dolan," he said.

I had to convince Gloria, if she hadn't already been convinced. "You've destroyed, or you're trying to destroy, everything you love. Isn't that right, Ringo? It's not an uncommon psychosis. Billy, for instance. It amused you to dominate her completely and to watch her gradual disintegration under the strain. She was completely under your thumb until I came along—isn't that right, Ringo? And then she started showing signs of fight, of rebellion, and so you simply hastened the inevitable destruction, got it over with in a hurry. You cut her throat."

Ringo's breathing was fast and hoarse. I spoke quickly. "And in my case. I was a real challenge to you, wasn't I, Ringo?"

His voice was thick. "You flatter yourself."

"I don't think so, Ringo. I spoke your language. You liked me and wanted to be liked by me. But principally you needed someone new to dominate, to smother with kindness or with fear or with your power, your money, your imagined superiority. But I wasn't duly impressed. You couldn't break me, in any way. You even went to the stupid length of finding Dusty, of taking her on, keeping her, waiting for a chance to rub my nose in the memory of her. Even that—when you finally got around to it—was a failure."

"He didn't tell me, Brad. I didn't know. I'd never have—"

I interrupted her. "I know that, Dusty." I turned back to Ringo. "I've been ahead of you all the way, Ringo!"

His smile was ugly. "You're forgetting one thing, Dolan. I'm ahead of you now, when it counts. You'll never leave this room alive!"

"Let me finish. When it became obvious to you that even your wife preferred me to you, you couldn't stand it any longer—"

Gloria sobbed.

I didn't want to look at her. "But you had to be the great manipulator. You had to do something clever, subtle, complex—like the way you tried to get rid of Sam Foster. In our case—Billy's and mine—to kill two birds with one stone. Get rid of Billy, hang the rap on me, and have your boys shoot me down in a faked jail break before the State could get me onto the witness stand. Very slick. Pull the strings and see the puppets jump! But your strings have tangled, Ringo. Your puppets are out of control and your show's a flop!"

I don't know why he didn't shoot me. Perhaps he was hearing the truth about himself for the first time and was perversely fascinated by it.

"And Gloria. You love Gloria perhaps more than anyone, anything you've ever had. And you have been smothering her. Destroying her. She's been like a girl in a trance around you, Ringo. All her normal emotions and reactions have been stifled, suffocated, by your domination. When she has been away from you she has been an entirely different person, Ringo. And let me tell you something that perhaps you don't know. I love her, Ringo. And she loves me. And I've held her in my arms—as close as any man can hold a woman—and when she is with me that way she is passionate and alive and everything that a beautiful and intelligent girl can be!"

Ringo's face blanched white. He stood, swaying, behind his desk. Spittle bubbled from a corner of his mouth. The muzzle of the Luger wavered slightly as his arm came up and forward. I stared at the muzzle, fascinated.

"Gloria," he muttered. "Do you believe these things he says about me?"

She was silent for a moment. She breathed deeply, harshly, and then, "Yes," she said.

I heard cars grind to a stop in the driveway. Then Dusty spoke, her voice hard, flat, emotionless: "You bastard. I was to be a part of your joke, your bad joke. And all those lies. 'I need you, Dusty. You're lovely and you're my kind of a woman and I need you. I don't care what you've been doing—none of us is perfect. I've made mistakes myself and perhaps the two of us together can put together the pieces of our lives and salvage something worthwhile. I need you, Dusty.' All those lies. I might have known."

She was moving across the room, moving toward him, moving in that long-legged, graceful, controlled swagger that I remembered so well. Her eyes were shining green, the way they always had when she had been emotionally upset, and she was, just for the moment, the Dusty Randall that I had known and loved.

"Stop, Dusty!" I shouted.

She crossed in front of me, walking toward Ringo, her eyes on the knife stuck in Ringo's desk. "It doesn't matter, Brad. It's much too late for anything to matter."

Ringo screamed, "You whore!"

She moved toward him, steadily. Someone was pounding on the door. I lunged for Dusty just as Ringo fired. My hands caught her around her waist, and as I dragged her to the floor I rolled and came to my knees between her and Ringo. And then I heard Carlton's voice behind me:

"Drop the gun, Ringo!"

Ringo's laughter was high and shrill. And then the still-smoking muzzle was in his mouth. *Gotterdammerung*, I remember thinking inanely. There should be mood music—a passage from *The Twilight of the Gods*. Gloria was moaning, "Stop him somebody stop him he's my father somebody please please stop him!" And then Ringo pulled the trigger. I watched him topple backward, back across the room, his great arms outstretched, against the rows of shelves behind his desk, then slump slowly to the floor, pulling books and records with him.

And then I was staring stupidly at the blood on my hands. I turned to Dusty Randall and saw the widening pool of blood on the rug by her side. Carlton was by her, reaching for her.

I shook my head at him. "I've got her, Carlton." He stood away and I sat beside her and lifted her head into my lap and she said, her voice a hoarse whisper, "I'm sorry Brad I couldn't help it it's the way I was ..."

"Hush. It doesn't matter. You're going to be all right."

She smiled at me, and then she died.

Carlton and his men asked their questions and made their notes and their phone calls. I stood still for the eating-out that Carlton gave me for running out on him at Ringo's fishing lodge, and for lousing things up, generally, and then Gloria and I walked through the strangely quiet house and onto the lawn. We walked, hand in hand, to the great banyan tree between the front door and the driveway. I held her close to me, and after a while she stopped sobbing and I kissed her long and tenderly. The great twisting branches of the banyan, the downward groping arms, were no longer frightening. Now they seemed to shelter us from evil.

THE END

William Fuller has born in Roxbury, Massachusetts, in 1913, and after two years of college, worked a variety of jobs, including freighter deckhand, migratory farm worker, short order cook,  Hollywood extra, newspaper reporter and publicity promoter. Fuller joined the army at the outset of World War II, and while stationed stateside, married Eunice Bourne Lee, heiress and stage actress, with whom he had three sons. After the war, the family moved to Winter Haven, Florida, where he began a career as a mainstream short story writer in 1946. Turning to crime novels in 1954, he wrote six Brad Dolan adventures in the 1950s, and one standalone novel, all for Dell Books. After retiring from his writing career, Fuller spent the rest of his life as the owner of a charter fishing boat. He died in Winter Haven in 1982.

Black Gat Books

Black Gat Books is a new line of mass market paperbacks introduced in 2015 by Stark House Press. New titles appear every other month, featuring the best in crime fiction reprints. Each book is size to 4.25" x 7", just like they used to be, and priced at $9.99 (1–31) and $10.99 (32–). Collect them all.

Stark House Press

1315 H Street, Eureka, CA 95501 707-498-3135
griffinskye3@sbcglobal.net www.starkhousepress.com
Available from your local bookstore or direct from the publisher.

Made in the USA
Monee, IL
30 July 2022